Barmy Jeffers dev ... n in life, as a mear ... r, Lauren. Not so l ... lo Walked into anotl ... y made several important friends and one important enemy, Baron Tanaka. The Baron had taken exception to Barmy destroying his fortress stronghold and was even now sending vampires to Barmy's real world to make him pay. For his own safety, he has no option but to return to the other world to settle with Baron Tanaka once and for all . . .

About the Author

J. H. Brennan is one of those peculiar people who seem to be living in several different worlds at once.

He has always been interested in magic, spells and wizardry and has written a number of books on magic. He is also the author of several Fantasy Role-Playing Games, including the highly successful *Grailquest* series published by Armada.

Barmy Jeffers and the
Quasimodo Walk

The Grailquest series

The Castle of Darkness
The Den of Dragons
The Gateway of Doom
Voyage of Terror
Kingdom of Horror
Realm of Chaos
Tomb of Nightmares
Legion of the Dead

Monster Horror Show

Horror Classics

Dracula's Castle
The Curse of Frankenstein

J. H. Brennan

Return of
Barmy Jeffers
and the
Quasimodo Walk

An Armada Original

First published in Armada in 1988

Armada is an imprint of the Children's Division,
part of the Collins Publishing Group
8 Grafton Street, London W1X 3LA

Printed and bound in Great Britain by
William Collins Sons & Co. Ltd, Glasgow

Chapter One

Sometime after Lauren and he came home again, Barmy Jeffers started getting weird dreams.

They all began the same way. He'd dream he was asleep in bed when something woke him. Then he'd dream he was lying there in the darkness of his room, eyes open, a little nervous, a little frightened, the way you are when something wakes you in the night.

And he'd listen.

At first the only thing he'd hear would be the thumping of his heart. Except after a while the beating of his heart would settle down and his legs would relax and the knot in his stomach would begin to untie itself and he would start drifting back to sleep, at which point he would dream there was a knocking at his window.

If he'd really been awake, of course, Barmy would have realized there couldn't be a knocking at his window, his room being on the second storey with absolutely no way anything bigger than a spider could climb up – something he knew from personal experience, having tried it often enough. So when he heard the knocking at his window, Barmy (in his dream) thought *there's something out there come to get me!*

Barmy had had thoughts like that quite a lot since the time he had managed to enter a different world. It was not that the experience had made him nervous but rather that his utterly incredible adventure had bred in him a definite streak of caution. When you've had to fight with ghouls and monsters, caution tends to develop very quickly. And in Barmy it had developed so firmly he had brought it home with him to his own world.

In the dream, Barmy would lie there for a long time, paralysed with fright, his heart really thumping, listening to the knocking, short and sharp, like somebody tapping a coin (or a claw – he kept thinking of claws) against the pane.

Eventually, in the dream, Barmy would remember he was the famous Quasimodo Walker who'd been through a Möbius warp, would recall he was a ghoul-slayer and slith-summoner, crusader against evil, friend of Ben and the Bong, at which point he would force his trembling limbs from between the sheets and would stumble, shivering, to the window.

He would stand there for a long time, gathering his courage, then slowly, nervelessly, his hand would reach out to draw back the curtain. In his dream he would hesitate, very much afraid, knowing there was something ghastly clinging to the outside wall, its hideous face pressed against the glass.

But his hand would move, of its own accord, to tug the cord which, inch by inch, edged back the heavy maroon drapes. He would watch the process with a sort of horrified fascination.

In the dream there was nothing at his window.

Six nights running he had the dream exactly like that. On the seventh night, while the rest of the dream was much the same, the ending turned out a little different.

He was standing at the curtain exactly as before, knowing, absolutely *knowing* there was something ghastly clinging to the outside wall, its hideous face pressed against the glass (but at the same time knowing there wasn't, since he remembered the earlier reruns of the dream). His hand went out exactly as before. The curtain drew back slowly, exactly as before.

6

There was something ghastly clinging to the outside wall, its hideous face pressed up against the glass. It was a tall, cloaked figure with skin so pale it might have been a corpse and eyes that burned and smouldered like a pair of glowing coals. Those eyes locked on Barmy's own and suddenly the creature smiled, drawing back thin, bloodless lips to reveal a set of fine, white teeth dominated by the most prominent canines Barmy had ever seen outside a zoo.

Dreaming or not, Barmy needed just two guesses to discover what this was. Either Hammer films were using this house as the set for their latest horror movie, or he was just one metre and a thin pane of glass away from the most feared of all dread legends, a living vampire.

For a timeless moment, nothing happened. The two were locked in static tableau, the towering black-cloaked, red-eyed, white-fanged creature just outside the window, and the boy Barmy, dressed in those stupid striped pyjamas his mother had picked out for him at some forgotten January sale. Barmy's heart raced like a new Ferrari, cold sweat broke upon his brow. He wanted to run, but his limbs staunchly refused to listen to the promptings of his head. He could not tear his eyes away, or even close them. Some magic of the moment forced him to stare into those glowing eyes . . .

Then, without warning, his paralysis was broken. He opened his mouth to scream and the right hand of the vampire smashed through the glass to seize him by the throat.

"Glug-glug," gasped Barmy, clawing at the vampire's arm. The thing had the strength of ten men, making him wonder briefly if it was a genuine vampire, or simply a homicidal maniac just back from the Rocky Horror Show. Either way, it was not a reassuring thought.

The vampire's smile widened and the muscles of its arm

rippled as it lifted Barmy bodily some half a metre off the floor, steely fingers tightening like a vice around his windpipe. Stupidly, Barmy noticed there were fine black hairs growing on the back of its hand. Equally stupidly, he also noticed that the fingers were cold, like meat.

Barmy's feet began to kick of their own accord and a red haze swam before his eyes. He could feel the growing tightness in his chest and the urge to draw another breath enlarged to fill his universe. It was proving a very vivid dream.

The creature outside laughed, a chill, mocking sound with not a hint of humour in it, which floated clearly into the room, partly because of the broken pane and partly because Barmy always slept with the top bit of the window open. After the first few dreams, he had considered sleeping with it closed, but decided he was being silly. Now, choking to death at the end of a vampire's arm, it didn't seem to matter much, one way or the other.

The hairy arm relaxed. Barmy felt his feet touch the ground and the pressure on his windpipe eased a fraction. He gulped air, twisted and bit down on the hand as hard as he was able. It tasted absolutely foul.

"Eeeeaaaaargh!" screamed the vampire, obviously unused to being bitten; and suddenly Barmy was free. He staggered back two steps, gasping, desperately hoping the shock might cause the monster to fall. But it still clung outside his window, sucking the back of its hand. The arm was badly lacerated from the remnants of the broken glass, but Barmy noticed there was no bleeding at all.

"Eeeeaaaaargh!" screamed the vampire again, this time in rage. It plunged its arm through the broken pane again, but now Barmy was sensibly out of range. At once the creature began to hurl itself against the window in a fury. The frame (which was of the old-fashioned wood type because nobody had ever got around to replacing it with aluminium) shivered and cracked alarmingly.

"Help!" Barmy yelled, except that the remnants of the brutal pressure on his throat caused it to come out as "Help!" in a squeak that would scarcely have done justice to a fieldmouse. He spun around and raced to the bedroom cupboard in search of a bat he could use as a weapon. He rummaged in a frenzy, trying desperately to ignore the noise of the enraged vampire at the window behind him.

It was soon obvious the only bat available was for table tennis and even that was broken, but he did find a sweeping brush his mother had stashed away as a broad hint that he should clean his room. He spun round and raced back to the window to poke the handle through the broken pane. It caught the vampire square amidships so that it fell away backwards with an explosive whoosh of expelled air.

For a moment the creature seemed to hang suspended in space, then the white, fanged face mercifully disappeared from view. Barmy leaped forward to press his nose against the pane, hoping to see a shattered form prostrate on the street below. But there was nothing, although he did think he caught just the barest glimpse of movement at the outer limit of the street lights, like the flicker of a long, black cloak.

A hand fell on his shoulder and Barmy jumped so violently he managed to crack his head quite badly against the wall. But it was only his sister Lauren, jeans and sweater pulled on hurriedly, peering at him myopically without her gold-rimmed glasses.

"What on earth do you think you're doing?" she asked him furiously. "You'll waken the entire house!"

"A va – a va – a va – " Barmy gibbered, pointing at the window.

9

She peered past him. "Look, you've broken the window! Did you do that with the broom?"

Barmy shook his head. "A va – " he said, massaging his throat and pointing.

"Oh for heaven's sake pull yourself together, Barney! Anyone would think you'd seen a – " she stopped suddenly, for reasons of her own.

"A vampire at the window," Barmy gasped. "Boy, what a bummer of a dream!"

"You're not dreaming now."

"No," Barmy agreed. His feet were freezing, his backside was cold and other details convinced him he was now fully awake. "I must have sleepwalked and – " He took a deep breath, knowing all confessions gave Lauren even more power over him, " – somehow broken the window."

But to his surprise, she shook her head. "I don't know if you sleepwalked, but you certainly didn't break that window."

"How do you know?" he asked, intrigued.

"The broken glass is on the inside," she told him smugly. "Whatever you were dreaming, there was definitely something out there trying to get in."

Barmy frowned. If there was any consolation for having a genius of a little sister, it was the fact she could often figure things out fast. "You think so?" he asked cautiously.

"I think more than that," said Lauren firmly. "I think there really was a vampire!"

Chapter Two

The house seemed deathly quiet, as if it were waiting with
bated breath for something horrible to happen. Barmy's
old man was off on another of his trips, sorting out some
software problems for the Saudis, but Barmy's mum was
there, three doors away, and Lauren's friend Emily was
downstairs on the sofa, and that ghastly, yappy little
pomeranian they were minding for Mrs Finklebaum was
lurking under something. There not a sound from any of
them. He recalled a late night movie he'd once seen
where every time the vampire called, a strange white mist
settled over the house and kept everybody asleep.

"Lauren . . ." he whispered nervously.

"Shut up, Barney," Lauren instructed him in her usual
ladylike manner. They were creeping across the landing,
the better to avoid waking their mother, Lauren in the
lead, which was the story of Barmy's life. She pushed
open the door to her room, in darkness except for the
reflection of the street lights outside, and gestured at him
impatiently.

As Barmy slipped inside, she closed the door carefully,
then snapped on the light. There was a man in leather
armour sitting on her bed.

Surprise caused Barmy's heart to leap into his mouth,
then recognition dawned. "Rowan! Good grief, it's
Rowan!" he exclaimed.

This takes a bit of explanation, not all of it believable.
The fact is, not so long before this night, Barmy messed
about with a thing he does (called the Quasimodo Walk,
because he walks like the Hunchback of Notre Dame) to

such an extent that he accidentally managed to pass through a sort of hole in the fabric of reality – called a Möbius Warp – and into a totally different dimension, another world, if you like, where there were monsters roaming loose and where magic worked.

In this other world, specifically in the Province of Magnum Varna, which is part of a country called Macanna, which in turn is part of an island chain called the Federated Isles of Skor, Barmy's sister Lauren got to be a war witch, while Barmy himself fought with ghouls and learned a bit of magic and made one important enemy.

Barmy also made several important friends – a dwarf called Ben, a lunatic called the Bong, a fighter called Facecrusher, a flamboyant Paladin called Pendragon, a wizard named the Amazing Presto, Aspen, the lethal love of his life, and a cheery little man who was by profession a thief. The thief's name was Rowan. And here he was now in Lauren's room.

"Rowan!" Barmy exclaimed, and turned to his sister. "Lauren, it's Rowan!"

"I know it's Rowan," Lauren told him crossly. "I can see it's Rowan. That's why I asked you to come in here."

She had in fact told him to come in, but he let it pass. "Rowan," he said, "how good to see you!" And in a moment of emotion, he went across and embraced Rowan fondly, for while they had not been particularly close friends, Rowan represented the whole of the Otherworld which Barmy had been missing.

"Nice to see you, too, Barmy," Rowan told him, grinning.

Barmy took a step back and felt his pyjama bottoms falling down. As he made a frenzied grab to retrieve them, Rowan handed back the pyjama cord. "Just practising," the thief said.

12

"What are you doing here?" Barmy asked. "How did you get here? When do you have to go back? How are the others? How's Ben? Lancie? How's Aspen? What happened after we left Baron – "

"If you could manage to stop rabbitting," Lauren said coolly, "Rowan might get a word in. He has something very important to tell you."

Barmy flashed her a poisonous look which failed to make the slightest impression. But he took her advice and shut up as he looked expectantly at Rowan.

"You remember Baron Tanaka?" Rowan asked.

"Do I remember Baron Tanaka?" Barmy echoed excitedly. He was only the one who had called up the slith that wrecked the Baron's castle. "Oh wow, do I remember Baron Tanaka! Do you remember those – "

"Take that as a 'yes'," Lauren put in crisply.

"The Baron didn't die when his castle collapsed," said Rowan soberly. "He wasn't seriously injured. In fact he wasn't even in the castle at the time. So he escaped without a scratch and made inquiries about who it was that caused him all the trouble. He's vowed eternal vengeance on every member of the party. For the rest of us that doesn't matter very much, so long as we keep out of the Wilderness Lands, which you wouldn't visit anyway unless you were well prepared for danger. But in your case, your's and Lauren's – "

Barmy blinked. "I'd have thought we were the safest of the lot – he can't get at us here: we're in a different world, for heaven's sake!"

Rowan shrugged. "Maybe. As against that, have you been having funny dreams?"

Barmy opened his mouth, then shut it again, as a small chill worm of fear began to work its way up his spine. "Funny you should ask that," he muttered.

"You have, haven't you?" Lauren put in. "You told me you were having funny dreams."

"Yes," Barmy confirmed. "Yes, I have."

"So have I," Lauren said.

Barmy rounded on her. "You never told me! I told you about my dreams and you never told me!"

"It was none of your business," Lauren said infuriatingly. "Please go on, Rowan."

"None of my bus – ?"

"The thing is," Rowan said.

"None of my busin – ?"

"The thing is," Rowan repeated more assertively, "in some ways it's easier to get at somebody in this world than it is to get at somebody stashed away safely in the Keep. I got here, didn't I?"

"How did you get here?" Barmy asked curiously. "Through one of Kendar's artificial warps?"

Rowan shook his head. "Kendar's disappeared again. We had to find a natural warp. We weren't sure where it might lead. So I came on account of thieves being able to get through when other people can't. I brought Eynek with me for protection and here I am."

Barmy made a mental note to find out who this Eynek person was, but for now he had a far more important question. "You mean Tanaka's likely to come through a warp as well?"

"Not personally, no. He's hired a hit vamp to take you out."

"Hit vamp?" Barmy echoed.

"Like a hit man, except this is a vampire," Lauren put in. "I assume that's what was knocking at your window."

Barmy swallowed hard, convinced he could again feel those cold, steely fingers on his throat.

"Vampires don't need to use warps, of course," Rowan said. "They have their own ways of getting from one

14

reality to another. That's what started
dreams."

For a moment nobody said anything. The
asked nobody in particular, "What are we going t

"I don't know what you're going to do," Laur͏ ͏d
him coolly, "but I have no plans to wait here quietly for
Tanaka's stupid vampire. I'm going back to Magnum
Varna to finish the job we started last time."

"You mean put paid to Tanaka?"

"That's what I mean," said Lauren firmly. And something in her tone swept aside the multitude of sensible
objections that were crowding Barmy's head.

"How do we get back?" he asked. "We can't use the
same warp Rowan did – they're strictly one way."

"You remember Kendar made an artificial warp to get
us home?" said Lauren.

Barmy nodded. "Yes."

"I watched what he was doing very carefully." She
walked over to her little built-in wardrobe and threw back
the door. Hanging inside in front of a rack of dresses was
a full-size Möbius strip, pegged to form an opening any of
them could walk through.

Barmy stared at it, suddenly seized by the old thrill of
impending adventure. "Will it work?" he breathed.

"Only one way to find out, isn't there?" Lauren told
him.

"I'll get my clothes," said Barmy promptly. He opened
the door and stepped on to the landing to find himself less
than half a metre away from the fiercest, largest and most
monstrous dog he had ever set eyes on. It looked something like a tan-coloured Irish wolfhound, but far broader,
with a thicker neck, deeper jaw and heavier muscles. It
wore a spiked collar and stood so high at the shoulder it
was able to look him directly in the eye.

Barmy staggered back two paces, his muscles turned to

...er, and he wondered why he'd found the vampire so frightening.

"I see you've met Eynek," Rowan's voice said cheerfully behind him.

Chapter Three

Their departure was messy.

"What about Mother?" Barmy asked.

"She's asleep," Lauren said.

It wasn't what he meant, but instead of pursuing the subject he asked, "What about Emily? Are you just going to leave her on the couch?"

"What do you want me to do – wake her up?"

"But what happens in the morning?"

"With any luck we'll be back by the morning," Lauren said impatiently.

There was actually a good chance she might be right. The last time they visited the Otherworld, they discovered time ran very differently there. On that occasion they had spent several weeks making a mortal enemy of Tanaka, only to discover no more than half an hour had passed when they returned back home. It was a freaky experience, but it had its advantages; not least the fact that nobody worried about you while you were gone. Lauren, who was into Relativity, was fascinated by the phenomenon and had already bent Barmy's ear ad nauseam with incomprehensible lectures about time streams and antimatter. In order to avoid sparking off another one, he changed tack again. "What about Poufé?"

Poufé was Mrs Finklebaum's ghastly pomeranian, a shampooed bundle of perfumed corruption which bit you when you looked the other way.

"What about Poufé?" Lauren asked frowning.

"What happens if he starts yapping in the night?"

"Let him yap," said Lauren shortly. She had put on her

glasses and was adding a coat to her sweater and jeans outfit lest the Otherworld proved cold.

"But if he wakes up Mother and she comes up to see what's happening she'll notice we're not here."

"Why should she come to your room or my room when Poufé's yapping in the kitchen?" Lauren asked.

"I was only asking," Barmy said. Eynek nudged him in the back so that he had to grasp Lauren's dressing table to avoid falling over. He turned and scratched the giant dog behind the ears. "What about . . ."

"What about? What about? What about?" hissed Lauren angrily. "All you can say is 'What about?' What about you taking time to plan what we're going to do about Baron Tanaka? He's the one who's sending vampires out to get us!"

"Me?" Barmy asked. "Why me?"

"You're the one with the sword and the armour," Lauren said, referring to their last trip when Barmy had indeed been dressed up as a warrior, however unsuited he had felt himself for that job. "You're the macho man who tries to rescue fair maidens from the ghouls." Which was a reference to the mess he'd made trying to rescue Aspen and, like most of Lauren's gibes, was unfair and far below the belt.

"What abou – " Barmy began as another point occurred to him. Then he thought better of it and fell silent.

"Are you sure that thing will work?" asked Rowan, nodding towards the Möbius strip pegged in the wardrobe.

"It's identical to the one Kendar made," Lauren said. She sounded confident, but Barmy knew her well enough to catch a defensive note in her voice.

"Kendar's a bit of a specialist," Rowan said, poking vaguely at the strip as if touching it would indicate how effective it might be. "Have you tried it out?"

"No," Lauren admitted. "Not actually tried it. I mean, there was no reason to before now and I feel so immature having to put on that stupid Quasimodo Walk . . ."

Barmy cheered a little at the mention of the Quasimodo Walk. It was his own invention entirely and it had enraged Lauren since she was a baby in her cot. Since it was also a necessity for travelling to the Otherworld, he now had a reason to practise it and irritate her frequently without her being able to protest. Sometimes life was almost sweet.

"The thing is," Rowan said, "these warps can be tricky."

"That was a double warp," Lauren pointed out.

"But I'm sure yours will work just fine. What do you say, Eynek?"

Eynek growled, a throaty sound like distant thunder, redolent with menace. Barmy stepped back in alarm.

"Just his way of talking," Rowan grinned. To Lauren he said, "All the same, it was a single warp that turned Pearl the Harper into a deathwatch beetle."

"You're making this up, aren't you?" Lauren said. She had a sharp nose for mick-takers having lived with Barmy all her life.

"Yes," Rowan said. "Are we ready to go?"

"Just about," said Lauren. She shrugged. "It's not like a spaceship. There are no buttons to press, no fine adjustments to make. So we just . . . do it."

Lauren turned to Rowan. "Barney will go first – "

"Why me?" Barmy protested. "Why should I be the one who has got to go fi – "

"Because you're the one who had most practice with that stupid Quasimodo Walk," Lauren explained with heavy patience. "It's the Walk that opens up the Möbius Gateway. We on the other hand, are not so skilled and might not manage it. So you go first with your Quasimodo

19

Walk and we will follow you, imitating the Walk as best we can." She smiled sweetly. "Okay?"

"What about Eynek?" Rowan asked. "He can't do a Quasimodo Walk. Can you, Eynek?"

Eynek growled.

"He doesn't have to," Lauren said. "Monsters can pass naturally through Möbius Warps."

Eynek growled again, more menacingly this time, the sound ending in a hideous snarl.

"What's the matter with him?" Lauren asked crossly.

"He didn't like you calling him a monster," Rowan said.

Barmy bent his left knee, curled his hands into claws, raised his right shoulder, trailed his right foot, shut his left eye, opened his right eye wide, curled his lips and started to move forward, breath hissing and wheezing, towards the wardrobe.

"That's what he does," Lauren explained unnecessarily. "That's his Quasimodo Walk."

But before he reached the loop, a rumpus on the landing caused him to straighten up. "What's that?" he asked in sudden alarm.

The answer rocketed into the room, yapping hysterically. "Oh Lor'," said Lauren, "Poufé's heard us! Shut him up before he wakes up Mother!"

"Fang, Eynek!" Rowan snapped.

"No!" shouted Barmy in alarm. He had visions of the massive Eynek eating Poufé alive.

"Hisssssssss!"

Poufé's yapping stopped abruptly.

"What happened?" Barmy asked. "What happened?" Poufé was running from the room, dripping like a drowned rat.

"Eynek peed on him," Rowan said. "That's the way he handles most things – he's a very peaceful dog."

20

"Come on," said Lauren, "let's get going before something else happens."

With Barmy in the lead, they Quasimodo Walked in a tight group towards the wardrobe.

Chapter Four

For a moment Barmy wondered if the warp had worked. He was in sudden darkness, admittedly, but that might have been due to somebody closing the wardrobe door. Certainly there was no indication anything else had happened: no falling sensation, no gut-wrenching moment of disorientation, no feeling of motion. There was one thing, though – the air smelt dry and musty with a hint of age, quite unlike the sort of air his fastidious little sister would permit inside her wardrobe.

There was no sound at all and for a hideous moment he knew with utter certainty he was alone. "Lauren?" he hissed in sudden panic. "Rowan?" Then in desperation, "Eynek?"

"Over here." It was Lauren's voice, steady enough except for a hint of suppressed excitement. She liked to play at being cool, but he suspected she enjoyed dangerous situations far more than he did.

"Is Rowan with you?"

"No," Lauren called. "Isn't he with you?"

"Rowan?" Barmy repeated. "Rowan?" He could see nothing in the darkness and was consequently afraid to move. To Lauren he said, "No, he's not with me. No sign of Eynek either."

"Mmmm," Lauren said unhelpfully.

The problem with Möbius Warps was that the space inside them was constantly changing. You could walk through one at noon and find yourself on top of a mountain. Walk through the same one ten minutes later and you might be in a desert several thousand miles away.

The first time Barmy Quasimodo Walked into the Other-world, he found himself wedged in among the branches of an oak tree. Lauren, who had entered the warp only a few seconds later, ended up in the Banqueting Hall of Castle Tanaka. If you went through as a group, close together, you had a reasonable expectation of everyone emerging in the same place. But it was not a certainty. That was the chance you took.

After a moment, Barmy asked, "What are we going to do?" His leadership potential was already slipping, but he didn't care. Lauren might be years his junior, but she had a better head for crises.

"Have you got a torch?" Lauren asked.

"No," Barmy admitted.

"Why not?"

"I didn't think to bring one," Barmy told her sourly. She had a knack for asking the sort of simple question that left him feeling stupid and vaguely guilty.

"Fortunately I did," said Lauren smugly. There was the faintest click and suddenly a beam of light cut through the darkness.

"Oh, an electric torch," said Barmy. "I didn't know you meant an electric torch." For some reason he had assumed she meant the sort of pitch-soaked torch in common use in the Otherworld. Not that he had thought to bring an electric torch either, as it happened.

The beam fell in a round pool on what appeared to be a flagstone floor. He waited for his eyes to adjust then discovered they were in a broad, stone-walled corridor, bone-dry, musty and with the dust of ages on its floor. Lauren moved the torch and the beam was swallowed in the darkness. She moved it again and the light danced and swung like a demented firefly.

"Where are we?" Barmy asked.

"How should I know?" Lauren snapped.

23

"Can't you keep the light steady?" Barmy muttered. But it was a token complaint. Now he knew he was not about to step over the brink of a precipice, he moved towards her with something approaching confidence.

Abruptly the light disappeared completely. Barmy stopped. "Lauren . . .?"

The light reappeared almost at once. "Come and look at this, Barmy." Her voice was small, but with a definite edge of excitement. Besides, she had called him Barmy which she almost never did unless she forgot herself completely.

He moved towards her. The light jumped and Barmy's heart lurched into his mouth. A hideous face was grinning at them, starkly picked out by the sudden illumination.

"It's all right," Lauren said. "It's only a statue or something. Come and look."

Barmy shuddered. "Wouldn't like to meet up with him on a dark night."

"There's something inside his mouth," Lauren said. "Can you see?"

"His tongue?"

"No, it looks like a lever. Can't you see – I'm not big enough?" She angled the torch so the beam fell squarely on the grinning mouth. Barmy squinted a little, but could see something remotely resembling a lever.

"No," he said.

"Yes, there is! Feel around inside!"

Barmy turned to stare at her in astonishment. "Feel around inside? That thing would bite my hand off!"

"It's only stone," Lauren said reasonably. "The lever might open up a secret door or something."

"If you think – " He stopped. There was something coming. Something big.

"Go on," Lauren urged.

"Listen!" Barmy hissed. The sounds were soft but

24

definite. Something was moving down the corridor towards them . . . and increasing its pace at the sound of their voices. Barmy suddenly realized both he and Lauren were completely unarmed. "Shine the light up ahead!" he urged to Lauren.

Lauren swung the light. The thing was closer than he thought. Barmy had a fleeting impression of a massive head and huge eyes before the creature was on top of him. He threw one arm up to protect himself and was slammed against the wall.

And licked.

And licked? He dropped the arm. "Eynek! Lauren, it's Eynek!"

"Grrrr!" said Eynek in agreement.

"Don't get him excited," Rowan's voice called from the darkness.

"Rowan?" Lauren swung the torch and picked him out, then politely pointed it downwards to show him where he was going. "How did you find your way without a light?"

"I followed Eynek. He used to be a guide dog for the blind." Rowan joined them. "Why doesn't your lamp smoke?"

"It's electric," Lauren said distractedly.

"Magic?"

"Sort of."

Rowan lost interest. "I'm glad Eynek sniffed you out. We could have lost each other forever in a place like this."

"Where are we?" Lauren asked. "Do you know?"

"In big trouble if we're where I think we are," Rowan said soberly. "Shine your light over here, Lauren."

She did so. Rowan was cradling in his hands a small, golden replica of a spider. It was exquisitely made, its eyes picked out in tiny gemstones.

"What is it?" Lauren breathed.

"Just what it looks like – a little golden spider. Quite precious as a work of art, but there must be a couple of dozen of them down the corridor. The point is, I can only think of one place where you would find these things. It's supposed to be just a legend, but everything about it fits. I think we've landed in the lost Tomb of Tarantulus."

"What's that?" asked Barmy, cautiously.

"It's supposed to be the most lethal location in the world," said Rowan. "There are things in here that make the southern Wilderness feel like a stroll through Bluebell Wood." He coughed. "Of course that's only a rumour. We can't be absolutely sure because no one's ever got out of it alive."

Chapter Five

Barmy, who was more nervous than lucid, said, "Tarantulus is that dangerous?"

"He's not dangerous at all," Rowan said. "He's been dead eight thousand years."

"It's a tomb, dummy!" Lauren said to Barmy. In the side-glow of the torch he could see her turn and simper infuriatingly at Rowan.

They were, at that precise moment, exploring the tomb in the hope of getting out of it. On an arbitrary decision, they had moved in the direction that Rowan had come from, past the little golden spider artifacts in the wall niches and were now approaching the source of a light seen distantly at the far end of the corridor. Nobody was getting excited. There was no way it could be daylight: the glow had a leprous green tinge about it, like luminescent fungus.

"Before the Federated Isles of Skor became federated, Tarantulus was King of Schemar, the northern island," Rowan said. "A very rich and powerful man on account of his spiders."

"Spiders?" Barmy echoed.

"He was what they call a webmaster," Rowan said. "It's a lost art now but Tarantulus had the gift and he was very, very good at training spiders," Rowan said.

"Training spiders? But what for?"

"You name it," Rowan said. "Spinning spider silk – light as a feather, but stronger than plate armour, although it's no good against a club. He started out with two spiders in a small back room and worked his way up to a whole chain of silk factories. Eventually he got so rich he bought the throne."

"He bought – ?"

"It's what they did in those days. But that was only the beginning. Of the spider business, I mean. He branched out into training them as message carriers and assassins – the poisonous ones, that is. He had his own spider guards. They say he was training spider soldiers, but he – "

"Spider soldiers?" Barmy asked, painfully aware he sounded like a bumpkin looking at the city lights.

"He learned how to grow them very big," Rowan said. "First about the size of a cocker spaniel, then later the size of a Great Dane. They know for sure he was trying to set up a spider army, but he died before he managed it."

"What of?" Lauren asked.

"Old age, I suppose."

"I just wondered if any of them bit him."

"Not Tarantulus," Rowan said. "Those things loved him. And vice versa, I suppose."

"What happened to them afterwards?" Barmy asked.

"What happened to who?"

"The spiders the size of cocker spaniels and all the rest – the jewel spiders and so on."

"I don't really know," Rowan said. "I suppose they died off. Once Tarantulus snuffed it, there was nobody with the skill to control them the way he had. And eventually, of course, the web arts died out altogether, over a few hundred or a few thousand years. Nobody knows them at all now."

"I assume," Lauren said, "King Tarantulus was very rich?"

"Well that's it, isn't it?" Rowan said. "Not just the richest king of his day, but reputed to be the richest ruler

28

in history. You can see why people were interested in finding his tomb."

"And nobody did?" Barmy asked.

Rowan chewed his bottom lip. "Difficult to say. Many parties went searching – it was one of the most popular adventure sports for centuries. Most of them came back without finding anything. But quite a few just . . . disappeared. The theory is they found the tomb, but didn't survive."

"Why wouldn't they survive, Rowan?" The light at the end of the corridor was growing stronger and Barmy, oddly enough, was growing more nervous.

"Kings in those days were very fussy about having their tombs robbed. The thing was to build your mausoleum, then surround it with so many traps and spells that any robbers are finished long before they find the family plate. Assuming they find your tomb in the first place, since you'd go to great pains to hide it away. The spells would mostly wear off in a few centuries, but a good mechanical trap can last forever."

"It's all a bit like our Egyptian Pharaohs," Lauren murmured. She seemed quite taken by the story.

"How do you know this is Tarantulus's tomb, Rowan?" Barmy asked.

"Well, I don't of course," said Rowan. "Not for sure. I don't really know where we've ended up. But all the legends talk about the little golden spiders he had made and I've never seen anything like these before – at least not so old."

"Grrr," Eynek said.

"Neither has Eynek," Rowan added.

The corridor ended in an archway which led directly into a high ceilinged chamber, illuminated by tens of thousands of tiny green glowing shards set into the walls. Overall, the light level remained dim, so they were left with the distinct impression of swimming underwater.

Near the wall directly opposite the archway was a tiered plinth on top of which stood a green marble statue of a muscular young man wearing a well-tailored fig leaf. He had short, tight-curled hair and pleasant, intelligent features. He stood, right leg crossed over left at the ankle, elbow leaning on a marble tree stump.

"Do you think that might be Tarantulus?" Barmy asked. There was no inscription on the plinth.

"I don't know," Rowan admitted. "I've only seen pictures of him as an old man. I suppose it could be, although I'd have thought if it was Tarantulus they'd have put a spider in the sculpture somewhere."

"There's a little one crawling up the log," Lauren remarked.

Barmy looked and found she was right. The insect had been carved with great subtlety and skill.

"Could be Tarantulus then, I suppose," Rowan said.

They looked around carefully. The only exit from the chamber was the arch through which they had entered. "No way out," said Rowan, as much to himself as to the others.

"Keep exploring?" Barmy suggested. Something in the back of his head had started to ask how long you stayed locked up in a tomb before you starved to death, but he managed to keep his voice steady. The others simply nodded.

They retraced their steps to the point in the corridor where they had originally met up, then continued to follow it in the direction opposite to that which had taken them to the green room. There were no branch corridors and after a hundred metres or so, it ended abruptly in a blank wall. Rowan knocked it carefully, but it rang with the dull note of solid stone.

For a moment nobody said anything, then Rowan remarked, "We're in a spot of bother. There doesn't seem to be any way out of here."

Chapter Six

'What do you think, Rowan?" Lauren asked. She held the torch a little higher.

They were standing in the corridor where Barmy and Lauren had first appeared, staring at the ghastly face cut into the wall. Lauren was back to her old obsession that there was a lever in its mouth.

"I think," Rowan said cautiously, "you might just be right." He tilted his head. "Yes, I think you are . . ."

"Secret door?" asked Barmy, who had been feeling left out of the proceedings.

"Could be," Rowan admitted. "I suppose there's only one way to find out."

"You're not going to put your hand in there?" Barmy gasped in sudden panic.

"No," said Rowan. "That would be a quick way to lose it at the elbow. You're going to put your hand in there."

"Ah me, ah I, ah hand, ah – "

"Just kidding," Rowan grinned. He opened the little leather sack he carried and drew out several steel rods which he jointed together expertly. "Tools of the trade," he explained briefly. "Stand well back both of you, and Lauren, try to shine your magic lamp straight into the mouth."

"Okay."

Barmy watched fascinated as Rowan carefully inserted the tip of the steel rod into the grinning mouth. There was a moment's pause, then he drove it forward in a short, sharp movement. At once the jaws snapped shut. The rod whiplashed briefly upwards, pulling out of

Rowan's hand and striking him a glancing blow across the nose, then clattered to the floor, the section within the mouth bitten off completely.

"Wow!" Barmy exclaimed.

A growling noise filled the air. Barmy glanced briefly at Eynek, then realized the sound was coming from the wall.

"I think I got it," Rowan said. "The lever." He did not sound entirely happy.

"What's happening?" Lauren asked.

The growling noise grew louder, now recognizable as machinery grinding deep within the walls.

"Well," said Rowan, "it could be a secret door as you suggest, Lauren. It could certainly be that. But then again, it could also be a hideous trap.

"What sort of hideous trap?" asked Barmy quickly.

"Shine your light straight up," Rowan said. Lauren complied. The ceiling was moving down to meet the floor at a sedate but constant pace. "That sort of hideous trap," said Rowan.

"What are we going to do now?" Barmy said quickly. Knowing Lauren, she would still be calmly discussing the situation while the ceiling squashed them like a set of bugs.

"Only one intelligent thing we can do," Rowan said.

"What's that?"

"Run like mad."

Together they bounded down the corridor in the direction of the statue room.

The entire corridor roof came down. They stood in a sorry little clump by the statue staring disconsolately at the archway, now sealed off by the lowered corridor, a wall of solid stone beyond all possibility of penetration.

So this is how it ends, thought Barmy. He had survived wolves and monsters, ghouls and varying degrees of hardship, not to mention his more recent run-in with a vampire, to end up the victim of a Möbius Warp that landed him inside the tomb of some dead king.

"I suppose we'll starve to death," he said to no one in particular.

"No fear of that," Lauren said promptly.

She had a plan! He knew she had a plan! Lauren was the smart one – she always had a plan! "Why won't we starve to death?" he asked. Eagerly.

"The air will run out long before that," Lauren told him. "Since the corridor came down, this chamber is hermetically sealed."

Rowan was systematically examining the walls, floor and ceiling, tapping here, prodding there.

"Any luck?" Barmy asked when he had completed a full circle.

"Not yet," said Rowan. He stared calculatingly at the statue. "But I haven't tried over there."

"Sorry?" Barmy asked.

"In my experience, you often find trap doors hidden under statues in a place like this. Or control mechanisms inside them. It's worth a try."

They walked across and Rowan tapped the statue. It sounded solid enough. "Push the plinth, Eynek," Rowan said.

"Grrr."

Eynek placed the flat top of his head against the plinth and pushed. The muscles of his neck and shoulders stood out like knotted ropes, but nothing else happened. He growled again and backed off.

"That's solid," Rowan said. "If Eynek can't move it, then it can't be moved. He's as strong as a horse."

There was a rumbling sound beneath their feet, the familiar grind of ancient machinery. "Strewth!" Rowan exclaimed. "He's started something up!"

34

"The corridor ceiling is starting to move up again!" Barmy yelled.

"Look at the statue!" Lauren called.

He glanced behind him. The young man in the fig leaf now had his back to the arch.

"Let's not get too excited," Lauren warned. "This is just the corridor opening up again. We still haven't found a way out of the tomb."

"Or further in," said Rowan.

"Further in?" echoed Barmy. "Why would we want to go further in?"

"To find the treasure of Tarantulus," said Rowan, grinning a little sheepishly. "You could retire for life on what you'd stuff into your pockets."

"I'd settle for just getting – " Barmy began, but was cut off by a deep throated warning growl from Eynek.

"What's the matter, Eynek?" Rowan asked quickly.

The archway was now half-open and the ceiling was still rising. Eynek trotted over to the opening and stood beside it, sniffing. Then he raised his great head and barked once.

"There's something coming," Rowan said and he drew a dagger from his boot, but Barmy noticed to his great surprise that Eynek's tail had begun to wag.

Chapter Seven

'What?" said a voice. "What? What? What? No squished bodies, no pancake corpses. I'd say that's a good sign, what?"

Barmy knew that voice! He could never forget that voice! The Reverend Lancelot Bong, one-time Secretary/Treasurer of the Borderlands Keep and all-time adventurer extraordinary.

But the figure who emerged from the archway was not the Reverend Bong. He was a powerfully-built, bearded dwarf attired in chain mail and with an ornate crossbow slung across his back. Eynek's tail began to spin like a propeller at the sight of him.

"Ben!" screamed Barmy and launched himself across the chamber floor.

"Hello, Eynek. Hello, Barmy. Hello, Rowan," Ben said carefully, greeting them in strict order of proximity. "Hello, Madam Obedniga." Madam Obedniga was Lauren by another name: the one she had used as a war witch.

Barmy embraced him fondly, patting the broad back and grinning like an idiot. Of all the friends he had made on his last adventure, Ben was by far the closest. "This is fantastic, Ben! How have you been? How did you get here? How did you find us? How did you get in? Can you get out?

A tall thin figure strode through the arch, attired in a full suit of plate armour that squeaked and rattled as he walked. His visor was pushed back, but even with it closed, the walk was unmistakable. This was definitely the

Bong. "Ah, there you are, Barmy, Lauren. Well done, Rowan. Get off, Eynek! Mission accomplished, what? All according to the motto, eh? Bless 'em, bash 'em, hack 'em, slash 'em!"

He was still talking when a very odd thing happened. A wooden rod, twenty centimetres long and glowing brightly at one end, floated through the archway as if carried by an invisible hand. Behind it walked a frowning man in white robes and a pointed hat. The rod swung and floated towards Rowan. It slowed as it reached him and hung in the air, the glowing tip some half a metre from his nose.

"Hello, Presto," Barmy said to the robed man.

"Barmy," Presto nodded briefly. But his attention was obviously still on the floating rod. "Well," he said to no one in particular, "it worked."

"Presto tuned a seeker rod on Rowan," the Bong explained, "in case you all got lost."

Two other figures emerged from the darkness of the corridor to step into the chamber, one broad, tall, muscular and ugly, a woollen cardigan pulled on over her metal breastplate, the other only a little taller than Barmy, with fair hair and a curious chained stone ball slung over her shoulder.

Barmy stopped pounding Ben's back to hug the larger of the two. "It's good to see you again, Facecrusher."

"Good to see you too, Barmy. Hello, Lauren – you're looking fit."

Barmy untangled himself and said shyly, "Hello, Aspen."

"Hello, Barmy. Good to have you back." Aspen grinned broadly at Lauren and moved to embrace her fondly. They had hit it off well together from their first meeting, rather to Barmy's chagrin since he felt a little jealous. Except now he felt nothing but pleasure: it was good to have the old group together again.

Or nearly. He looked around. "Where's Pendragon? Isn't he with you?"

"He's outside," Lancelot explained. "When the secret passage opened, he started to argue about whether we should come in, so we left him there."

"There's a way out?" The question came from Lauren, who seldom missed much.

"The same way we came in, Madam Obedniga," Ben said. He reached up to pat Eynek who was licking the top of his head.

"How did you come in?" Barmy asked the Reverend Bong.

"With great difficulty, Barmy. To tell the truth, we were still looking for an entrance when one opened up of its own accord. Presto's seeker indicated you were inside, so we assumed you must have opened it. Except for Pendragon, of course. He assumed it was opened by something dangerous. We left him arguing with himself and the rest of us came in tally-ho. How did you open the passage by the way?"

"I think," Lauren put in, "we should make our way out. Since we don't really know how the passage opened, we don't really know how long it's likely to stay open."

"Yes," Presto agreed. He looked round warily. "There's a smell of ancient magic about this place. That's always tricky. Once spells start to crumble, you never know what's going to happen."

The exit passage had opened just beyond the spot where the stone face had bitten Rowan's rod. Although Barmy felt a little nervous as he passed through it, the way remained open as each of them came out, eyes blinking in green filtered sunlight. In stark contrast to the dry and musty interior, they emerged into a steam-bath atmosphere, redolent with the most exotic smells. They seemed to be in a clearing in a jungle full of ferns and broad-leafed grasses.

Barmy turned to look where he had been and discovered the tomb to be a massive sandstone pyramid, solidly constructed with the largest building blocks he had ever seen. As his eyes were drawn upwards, he noticed a curious flickering at the apex, subtle but distinct, like electrical fire. The immediate surround of the pyramid was barren of plants, except for a little lawn-like area of short grass – a surprising situation for something so old: he thought the jungle would have overgrown it completely by now.

"Where are we?" he asked.

"Not far from home, funnily enough," the Reverend Bong said. "A small island off the coast of Macanna."

"But this is tropical," Lauren protested. Like Barmy, she recalled Macanna as fairly temperate, even a little cold.

"Volcanic," the Bong said. "Peculiar little place. It's full of hot springs and steam vents and mud lakes on the boil. Geysers and so forth. There's so much heat and moisture it feels tropical. Even the plants are fooled: you won't see vegetation like this for nearly two thousand kilometres due south."

"Where I come from," Barmy said, "they'd build a hotel here and set the whole place up as a holiday resort."

"Where I come from too," the Bong said. "Might be tempted to make a small investment in it myself, what?"

"Why hasn't it happened, Lancie?"

"What – the hotel and holiday resort? Nobody knew the island was here until we found it."

"But I thought you said it was near the coast," Barmy said.

"Near the coast and hidden by a permanent fog bank –

39

volcanic activity again, of course. It's not on a shipping lane, not on the way to anywhere, no reason why anybody should explore it, no – "

"What a place to hide the tomb!" Rowan exclaimed half to himself, his eyes wide with admiration.

"What? What What?"

"Do you know what this place is?" Rowan asked excitedly. He made a broad sweeping gesture with his right arm to take in the totality of the pyramid. "Do you know what this wonderful, marvellous, incredible place is? This is the Lost Tomb of Tarantulus!" Rowan screamed excitedly. "And we've found it! We're rich! All of us! We're rich! Rich, I tell you! Filthy, stinking rich!"

"That's good, Rowan," Ben said.

"There's only one problem . . ." It was a new voice. Barmy turned to see Pendragon approaching, leading a small train of horses. His armour, as always, was brightly polished and he looked more stunningly handsome than ever.

"What's that, Draggie?" Ben asked.

"If that really is the Tomb of Tarantulus, the treasure is somewhere inside it. And nobody – " He paused dramatically, ". . . nobody has ever come out of it alive!" He looked earnestly from one face to another, his own features set in a grim, emphatic mask. Aspen rolled her eyes briefly towards heaven.

"We could do it!" Rowan said, ignoring him. "Now the old team's together, we could loot this place stupid. We destroyed Tanaka's Castle – they said that couldn't be done. This will be a doddle by comparison. We'll be famous. The first adventure party to find the Lost Tomb of Tarantulus and live! More to the point, we'll be rich! We can have castles and servants. We can have rooms full of gems. We can have solid gold baths. Eynek can have a diamond studded collar – "

"Grrr," said Eynek enthusiastically.

"We can have the best – "

"Actually," Lancelot Bong put in, "there is one other smallish problem . . . Baron Tanaka."

"He sent a vampire after us," Lauren said in a tone of sudden outrage. "A hit vamp!"

"Yes, I know," the Bong nodded. "That's why we sent Rowan to find you. But he's done a great deal worse than that since you left, Rowan."

Something in his tone stilled Rowan's excitement. "What's he done, Lancie?" he asked quietly.

"He's cracked our defences."

For a chilling moment there was silence. Then Rowan asked, "How?"

"According to my information, he's managed to smuggle a whole crypt of vampires right into the Keep. They're hidden somewhere inside at this very moment."

"How many?"

"I think seven," said the Bong, "but that might not be correct."

"What's he planning to do?" Barmy asked. The Borderlands Keep was the bastion that kept the wasteland monsters from invading the fertile north of Macanna.

"He's raising a ghoul army," put in Facecrusher. "Ghouls and anything else he can persuade to follow him. He's going to attack the Keep in force."

"But that's really only a diversion," Aspen said.

The Bong nodded. "The real plan is to turn the vampires loose while everyone's attention is diverted. Since they infect anyone they bite, half the ruling Council of the Keep could be vampires themselves – and under Tanaka's power – by morning. You can imagine what that would mean."

"Yes!" Barmy breathed.

"So you see why we can't hang around to loot the tomb, Rowan," the Bong said briskly.

"When is the attack planned?" Barmy asked. "Do you know?"

"The weekend," said Facecrusher. "If we're to find the vampires before then, there's not a moment to lose."

Chapter Eight

It was like coming home. The boat trip from the island took less than an hour and the march across Macanna less than two days, but when Barmy entered the Valley of the Fortress his excitement began to rise like that of a thirsty horse with its first scent of distant water. And when he saw the great Keep itself, guarding the pass – the only pass – to the Badlands and Tanaka's realm, his heart leapt.

As they trotted towards the main gate, where the portly figure of the Mayor headed an entourage which had emerged to greet them, Barmy said quietly to Face-crusher, who was riding beside him, "How many people know about the vampires, Facecrusher?"

"Only us," Facecrusher told him softly.

"How come?"

"Lancelot was worried about causing panic if the word got out. Well you would, wouldn't you, knowing you were living in the same Keep as a nest of vampires?"

Barmy, who was panicking a bit already, nodded.

"The trouble is," said Facecrusher, "the only thing you can do in a situation like this is search out the vampires and stake them. You don't need an army for that and a terrified population only gets in the way. When Lancelot found out, he thought we were best equipped to do the job. So we're the only ones he told."

"How did he find out?" Barmy asked.

"The Church Militant has its own Intelligence Service," Facecrusher said. "Very big in espionage."

"Bless 'em, bash 'em, hack 'em, slash 'em and spy on 'em!" Barmy grinned.

Facecrusher smiled. "Something like that."

From the walls above the main gate, a brass band struck up, launching into a tuneless march. A ragged cheer broke out from a small group of onlookers who had drifted out to rubberneck the proceedings. The Mayor walked forward briskly for a man of his bulk, stopped before the Reverend Bong's horse and said formally, "The Keep salutes Your Holiness and welcomes the return of the brave adventure party whose courageous exploits are an example to us all." He cast a jaundiced eye towards the Amazing Presto, an old enemy, but bestowed a benevolent beam on the rest, with the exception of Eynek whose fearsome appearance caused a wary expression to pass across his face.

"Grrr!" said Eynek suddenly, presumably because the dislike was mutual.

"My party and I thank you, Your Worship, for your generous words and welcome," the Bong replied with equal formality.

The Mayor looked around, "It is my duty and my pleasure to invite each and every one of you to attend a state banquet in the Town Hall tomorrow evening." The voice dropped. "Except for the mutt, of course."

"Grrr," snarled Eynek, who had very good hearing.

"I thank you on behalf of my colleagues and myself," the Reverend Lancelot said grandly, "and accept your kind invitation with pleasure." He too dropped his voice. "Now can we cut this short – everybody wants a hot bath and a good lie down."

The Mayor bustled from one party member to the other with every indication of goodwill. "Aspen isn't it? How nice to see you . . . And you must be Lauren Jeffers, or should I call you Obedniga, ha-ha . . . And Ben – still

44

keeping the old crossbow oiled, eh? . . . How do you do, Rowan. I see you've got yourself a little doggie – "

"Grrr!" snarled Eynek again, a sound so threatening that it chilled the blood.

"Lady Tanaka," said the Mayor, bowing effusively to Facecrusher. "Nice to see you." He turned. "And you must be the famous Barmy Jeffers – slith-summoner extraordinary!"

Barmy, who did not feel famous, gave an embarrassed smile and took the proffered hand.

The brass band was still playing (badly) as the formalities ended and they swept through the main gate into the outer courtyard of the Keep.

"Glad that's over," Lancie Bong said fervently. "Right. Barmy, you and Lauren are my guests, so you come with me. The rest of you go off and do whatever you have to do and I suggest we all meet up at the *Pig and Dragon* tavern around three o'clock." He dropped his voice and looked around suspiciously. "For a briefing."

"What's the matter, Barmy?" Ben asked quietly. "You look as if you've swallowed a rat."

"I don't know, Ben," Barmy said uncertainly. He chewed his lower lip. "How well do you know the Mayor?"

"Very intimately," Ben said.

"What's that mean?"

"What's happened, Barney?" Lauren asked sharply, her earlier irritation suddenly replaced by interest.

"I don't know . . ." Barmy said thoughtfully. "It could be nothing . . ."

"Well, tell us!" Lauren demanded. "You're infuriating in this wishy-washy mood."

"Barmy isn't wishy-washy, Lauren," Ben said. "He just seems – "

"I was just wondering if his hands were always so cold,"

Barmy said. "The Mayor. Do you know if he has particularly cold hands?"

"Not usually," the Bong said thoughtfully. "Although now you mention it, he did feel a bit chilly when we were shaking hands today."

"That's when I noticed it," Barmy said. "It's probably nothing at all," he said uncomfortably. "It's just that the last hand I felt as cold as that belonged to the vampire the Baron sent to get me."

Chapter Nine

"You think he might be?" Aspen asked.

"Wouldn't put it past him," muttered the Amazing Presto. "I never liked that man."

"You're being unfair, Presto – you know that?" Face-crusher said. "You're being very unfair. If he *is* a vampire, it's because he's been bitten. It's not something that's his own fault: it's something that could happen to any of us."

They were gathered together in the living room of the Reverend Bong's large but somewhat crumbling home, discussing the situation and taking turns for hot baths.

"But is he a vampire?" Pendragon asked rhetorically. "That's precisely the point. I mean, so he's got cold hands – so what? Maybe he just forgot to wear his gloves."

"Eynek thought there was something wrong with him," Barmy said.

"Grrr," Eynek confirmed. He was stretched out before the fire, taking up all of the hearthrug and absorbing most of the heat.

Rowan scratched the side of his nose. "I thought that was a bit odd myself. Eynek's usually such a friendly dog."

"That's right," Lancie Bong agreed. "And old Harry usually gets on quite well with just about everybody and everything, whatever Presto might tell you. Anybody notice his teeth?"

"There was nothing wrong with his teeth," Aspen said. "He smiled a lot and there was nothing wrong with them."

"That's what I thought," said the Bong. "Of course, that doesn't prove anything one way or the other."

"What do you mean, Lancie?" Ben asked.

Lauren entered the room wearing a bathrobe and towelling her hair. "What he means is that you don't turn into a fully-fledged vampire all at once, even if you are bitten."

Barmy sighed inwardly. He was so sick of Lauren's expertise in everything. Now it looked as though she knew about vampires as well. And the really sickening thing about her was that she was always so accurate, so right. Or nearly always . . .

"It's like an infection," Lauren was explaining. She pushed at Eynek's rump to make space at the fire so she could dry her hair. To Barmy's secret delight, Eynek refused to move. "It takes hold quite gradually. If the Mayor has been bitten, he'll go over to the bad guys immediately. He'll develop a taste for fanging people right away, but he'll still be able to pretend he's normal for quite a long time."

"Move over Eynek!" Lauren snapped irritably. Eynek turned his head to look at her balefully, but otherwise remained immobile. "What I mean is he won't show any signs, any definitive signs, for anything up to a week or ten days. His eyeteeth won't stay long when he isn't actually fanging somebody and as you've noticed, he's still quite capable of coming out in daylight without discomfort. Will somebody help me move this brute – I need to dry my hair."

"Grrr," Eynek said.

"He'll never move now," Rowan said. "Not now you've called him a brute."

"Oh spit!" Lauren snapped.

"What Lauren says is quite correct," the Reverend Bong said cheerfully. "If old Harry has gone over to the opposition, there's no way we can be absolutely sure until he starts to fang somebody himself."

48

"The thing is," said Lauren thoughtfully, "if we can kill the vampire who fanged him before it goes too far, we can stop the Mayor turning into a vampire permanently."

"That would be worth doing," said the Bong emphatically. "Old Harry's not such a bad stick when you get to know him."

The Amazing Presto sniffed, but had the good grace to say nothing.

"I don't like this state banquet business," Aspen said suddenly. They turned to look at her. "Think about it," she told them defensively. "This vampire business hasn't come up out of the blue. Tanaka's behind it – we all know that. He's sent one vampire to get Barmy and Lauren and he's sneaked heaven knows how many more into the Keep. He wants to break out of the wastelands, we all know that. But what else does he want?" She looked from face to face.

"What else does he want, Aspen?" Ben asked. "You tell us."

"He wants us." It was not Aspen who spoke but Facecrusher. "That's obvious. We're the ones who demolished his castle and buried his rotten monster collection. Of course he wants us. He wants us to die in the most cruel, horrible, terrible, slow – "

"That's what I thought," said Aspen. "And what better way to get us all together than at a banquet? We're all invited."

"Grrr."

"Except you, Eynek. And Eynek wasn't involved in wrecking his rotten castle."

"Besides which," put in Barmy, "I think Eynek was very suspicious about the Mayor."

"Grrr," Eynek said.

"It certainly begins to make a horrid sort of sense," Lancelot admitted.

"The question is," Lauren put in, "what do we do about it?"

"I think we should follow the Mayor, Lancie."

There was total silence for a moment while everyone looked at Ben in something close to amazement.

"What a brilliant idea!" Lauren exclaimed at length. "What an absolutely splendid notion."

Frowning, Barmy said, "If he has been bitten, the chances are he will lead us right to wherever it is the other vampires are hiding out."

"I know," added Lancelot Bong with great delight. "We'll all follow in disguise."

Chapter Ten

"This is crazy!" Barmy whispered.

"You can say that again," Lauren muttered angrily. She was wearing an ankle-length smock dress of a cut and style that went out of fashion shortly before Noah found landing space for the Ark. The dress was topped by an apron which bore the legend *Goodwife Biddle* and a huge, floppy bonnet, tied at the chin, which left most of her face in shadow. She was pushing a large pram, of the type matrons used to walk triplets.

Barmy managed to look even sillier, since he too wore a bonnet and was in the pram. Underneath an almost unbelievably ticklish blanket of soft, pink wool, he wore only an oversized nappy and boots. Inside the pram was a bundle of sharpened wood stakes, two daggers and a sword.

They were proceeding through the market square: the same square in which Amazing Presto had once unleashed an irate slith. It was late afternoon now and while the square was far from deserted, it was not actually bustling with business either. About a third of the stallholders and vendors had packed up for the day and those who remained had only a few customers.

Up ahead, the Mayor was purchasing a ceramic jar full of olive oil.

At this stage, Barmy was beginning to have serious doubts about his earlier suspicions. Cold hands or not, he had been behaving with every indication of normality since they had begun to track him following his departure from the Town Hall.

His official duties were obviously over for the day, for he had abandoned his mayoral robes and chain in favour of dun brown doublet and breeches and strong leather boots. He had topped this outfit with a jaunty little Robin Hood hat, complete with feather, and was now strolling through the Keep, smiling at his constituents and patting small children on the head.

It was a very long time since Barmy had seen anything that looked less like a vampire.

"Thank you, Mr Brocklehurst," the merchant said fawningly, the result of having been instructed to keep the change. "Thank you very much indeed, sir."

Mayor Brocklehurst grinned amiably (and there was *still* nothing wrong with his teeth), stowed away the jar of olive oil and continued with his stroll.

"Do you really think this is going to do any good?" Barmy was having second thoughts.

"No," Lauren hissed back, "but I think we're stuck with it." She sniffed. "Thanks to you. You got us into this!" Lauren told him furiously. "You kept going on and on about his stupid hands as if people – "

"I didn't go on and on," Barmy protested. "I simply mentioned – "

"Good grief," Lauren said, "he's coming this way!" She swung the pram around abruptly and headed full tilt behind a stall. Barmy, who had been shifting position when she made the move, was flung into the bottom of the pram, cracking his head and bruising his shoulder. As he climbed back into a sitting position, he caught a brief glimpse of a smallish group of entertainers – two clowns, a dancing bear and a pantomime horse – picking out a space from which to amuse what was left of the crowd. It occurred to him that none of this was real; that he was asleep and dreaming in reaction to a pizza supper. He rubbed his head, where a bump was already forming. He had once fought a congregation of ghouls who did him less damage than this.

He half turned to give Lauren the benefit of an angry protest, then shut his mouth abruptly. The Mayor had circled round the stall from the other direction and was bearing down on them.

He stopped and raised his hat to Lauren. "Ah, Goodwife . . ." He squinted at the legend on her apron. "Biddle, isn't it? I don't believe we've met. I'm Harold Brocklehurst – Mayor Brocklehurst, that is, although everybody calls me Harry, especially coming up to election time, ha-ha! Might I ask if you are new to our little community?"

"Oh ahr," Lauren said, in a very passable imitation of an idiot bumpkin.

"Well, I'm certain you will like it here," the Mayor said, having obviously taken Lauren's short outburst of rolling rubbish to be an affirmative answer. "Even though we play a vital part in safeguarding the welfare of our glorious realm, it is in fact extremely peaceful here."

"Aghr," Lauren acknowledged, turning her head away slightly, a manoeuvre which made her look more like an idiot than ever.

"Of course the Civilian Administration – of which I have the honour to be the head – has a great deal to do with that," said the Mayor, smiling benignly, "as I sincerely trust you will remember at election time."

"Ahr," said Lauren shortly; and this time the sound bore a distinct resemblance to Eynek's most vicious snarl.

But like most politicians, the Mayor seemed to be immune to subtleties. "And what a pretty baby!" he gushed turning his attention to the horrified Barmy. "Is it a little boy or a little girl?"

"Aghr igle aghr," Lauren rumbled.

"Ah, a little girl!" exclaimed Mayor Brocklehurst,

eyeing the pink blanket. He reached underneath and tickled Barmy's naked stomach. "Coochie-coochie-coo! Coochie-coochie-coo!" His hand still felt cold, like meat.

It was very quiet in the space behind the stall. More and more of the merchants were packing up, more and more of their customers were drifting away. Shadows were lengthening as the winter sun dropped behind the rooftops of the houses circling the market square.

"So delightful at that age," the Mayor said. "So rosy. So plump. So . . . tender . . ." His tongue flicked out to lick his lips.

"Oh aghr, ghar dur worzle," Lauren muttered, mercifully swinging the pram out of the Mayor's chill reach and indicating by body language, if not by words, that she really had to be getting on.

"Not . . . so fast!" said the Mayor coolly; and suddenly there was a hardness in his face that had not been there before. He smiled and somehow the smile did not reach his eyes. "You really must allow me to walk you home, my dear. It is getting dark . . ."

Which was all too true. Barmy flicked a quick glance around him to discover the market square was now virtually deserted, its empty stalls standing like skeletons in the growing dusk. It had all happened with disturbing speed.

"I can walk myself home, thank you very much!" Lauren said distinctly, her voice emerging from the depths of her stupid bonnet like a snake.

But if Mayor Brocklehurst was surprised by the sudden transition, he did not show it. "But my dear, you never know what you might meet when the sun goes down." His smile broadened.

It might have been a trick of the light, but to Barmy his teeth looked longer.

"Get out of my way, you grot-faced tub of lard!" said

Lauren, who tended not to mince her words when her temper finally broke. She swung the pram again, this time using it as a sort of battering ram. The vehicle crashed against the Mayor's legs and stopped dead, as if it had hit a solid wall. Barmy pitched forward and cracked his head again.

"Careful of the baby," Brocklehurst said softly. His teeth were definitely longer and his fat face seemed curiously leaner. "We wouldn't like to damage such a plump, tender . . . morsel!"

He leaned over the pram and his eyes glowed red. Those elongated teeth were less than half a metre from Barmy's throat.

"No," Brocklehurst repeated, "we wouldn't want to damage a tasty little bite like this . . ."

Chapter Eleven

Barmy's nerve broke and he leaped out of the pram, wrapping the pink blanket around himself in a lunatic sweep of modesty. With amazing presence of mind, he gripped the sword en route, so that he landed cat-like in the market square in a full fighting stance. Out of the corner of his eye, he saw Lauren sweep back her bonnet and draw something from a pocket of the apron.

"Well, well," said Brocklehurst with not the least hint of surprise. "A remarkably large baby, if I may say so, Goodwife Biddle . . . or should I say Mistress Jeffers!"

"So you knew," Lauren muttered.

"Knew?" Mayor Brocklehurst threw back his head and laughed ironically. "Knew? Of course I knew! You don't imagine those ludicrous outfits fooled me for a moment. I spotted you the second I left the Town Hall; only I was in no position to do anything about it . . . until now!"

In the last rays of the setting sun, his face seemed actually to writhe, the plump and rather pleasing features replaced by sharper, harder planes. There was no longer the slightest doubt about his teeth, two of which now protruded so alarmingly that they hung down over his lower lip. His body too was changing, elongating, growing leaner, more muscular and threatening. Barmy noticed the ring finger of each hand was now a shade longer than the index finger.

"Back off!" Barmy said grimly, brandishing his sword.

Slowly the Vampire Mayor advanced towards him, smiling. Barmy feinted twice without so much as a flicker from the Mayor before a horrid realization dawned.

Swords – or any other metal weapon – were supposed to be more or less useless against vampires. The only thing that could kill them properly was wood, hence the stake through the heart.

And the only thing that was supposed to keep them at a distance was garlic which, of course, he had not thought to bring.

But there were stakes in the pram!

He lunged towards it, but fast as he was, the Vampire Mayor was faster, leaping with lightning-like rapidity to land between Barmy and his sister and her pram.

"Forgotten something, have we?" the Mayor asked lightly. "Our soother, perhaps? Or our bottle? Or something a little more . . . deadly?"

"Mr Mayor . . ." said Lauren.

"Shut up, little girl – I have business with your brother."

Barmy chilled, as much in anticipation of Lauren's reaction to the term "little girl" as in fear of anything the creature could do to him. Although he was not exactly happy about what the creature could do to him either. None of this was going right. The plan had been to follow the Mayor until he led them to Tanaka's vampires. Then Tanaka's vampires were to be staked which would, hopefully, release the Mayor from his horrid bondage, allowing him to revert back to normality.

Nobody had anticipated a hassle with the Mayor in the middle of a deserted market square. Barmy wondered what would happen if he hacked the Mayor with his sword, despite the rumours that metal would not work.

"Mr Mayor . . ." said Lauren again, sweetly.

"What is it, little – " The Mayor half turned, then stopped, eyes ablaze. Lauren was holding a string of garlic bulbs in her right hand, swinging it gently as one might swing a chained mace or a whip.

"You heard my brother, Mr Mayor," hissed Lauren.

57

"Back off!" She stepped towards him and made a threatening gesture with her garlic string.

To Barmy's inexpressible horror, the Vampire Mayor reached out and grabbed the garlic string. He smiled terribly at Lauren, then bit vigorously into a bulb. The pungent scent of garlic filled the air.

"It only works in your world, little girl," he said.

Barmy found his mind was racing like an engine. If it only worked in her world – his world – their world – maybe the other stuff was different here as well. Maybe metal wasn't useless against vampires. Maybe –

Nobody had mentioned garlic, but both the Bong and Presto had told him never to rely on metal. Maybe they hadn't mentioned garlic because they –

He was getting himself confused. The Vampire Mayor was moving with ghastly deliberation towards Lauren. He had to try whatever was to hand. He swung the sword. "The stakes!" he called to Lauren. "Get the stakes!"

The blade hissed in a deadly arc – and missed, not through any vampiric peculiarity but because the hairy-legged boy with the scarf he had noticed earlier appeared out of nowhere and cannoned into him. Barmy stumbled sideways.

Lauren lunged forward with the pram, ignoring Barmy's instruction about the stakes. The vampire made a dramatic sweeping gesture with his arm and brushed it aside. The pram tumbled end over end, spilling stakes and daggers.

A looming shape appeared behind Lauren and Barmy groaned inwardly. As if they weren't in more than enough trouble already, the performing bear had broken loose.

"Behind you!" he called desperately. But Lauren was mesmerised by the vampire.

Another figure abruptly appeared on the scene – the tall, fat woman with the creaking stays; possibly, Barmy thought, the hairy-legged boy's mother. She ploughed in like a battleship, somehow ending up between the Vampire Mayor and Lauren. Before Barmy could even shout another warning, the vampire lunged forward and bit her in the shoulder.

And screamed!

"Tally-ho!" exclaimed the tall woman, swinging her handbag to catch the vampire on the ear. The creature staggered back, clasping its ear with one hand and covering its mouth with the other. "Bless 'em, bash 'em, hack 'em, slash 'em!" screamed the woman.

Lancie? Barmy twisted to see. He'd shaved his beard and padded his body, but . . .

The small boy with the hairy legs ran forward, head down, to butt the vampire in the stomach. At the moment of impact, the boy's scarf slipped to reveal a heavy black beard. "Take that, Harry," he told the Vampire Mayor in slow, familiar tones.

The bear, Barmy thought, the bear! "Lauren!" he screamed again. "Behind you!" But the bear was lumbering past Lauren, headed for the vampire. As it passed Barmy, Pendragon's voice remarked conversationally, "It's all right, Barmy, it's only me."

"Alive!" called the heavily disguised Lancie. "We have to take him alive!"

Which was possibly easier said than done, since the Vampire Mayor had now recovered from his earlier surprise and was casting about for an escape route.

Lancelot Bong jumped forward noisily. The creaking sounds were obviously not his stays, but as Barmy now recognized, plate armour worn beneath his dress. No wonder the vampire had done itself a mischief trying to bite his shoulder. But, armoured and padded as he was, the Bong moved slowly so that the monster dodged past him and crashed into the bear-suited Pendragon.

Caught off balance, Pendragon fell back a step, but aimed a sweeping kick at Brocklehurst's legs. Had it connected squarely, the Vampire Mayor would have been down, but the blow was a glancing one so that the creature only staggered.

Barmy could see two other figures racing to the scene – the two clowns from the entertainment troupe, presumably in pursuit of their dancing bear.

Except that their dancing bear was actually Pendragon in . . .

Barmy saw they were carrying a net and his heart leaped. The larger had to be Facecrusher, the smaller Rowan. Which would make sense, since the Amazing Presto would be inclined to stay outside any physical hassle in order to throw spells if needed. What a strategy! What a team!

"What a mess!" Lauren exclaimed.

She was right. Lancelot had managed to trip over Ben and both were now prostrate on the ground. The Vampire Mayor jumped over them and threw one arm around Lauren's throat. He began to walk backwards, dragging her with him. "One more move and the girl gets it!" he shouted like the heavy in a thriller movie.

Unaccustomed to playing victim, Lauren twisted round to bite his arm while simultaneously driving her elbow back into his ribs and stamping viciously on his instep with her heel.

"Oooowooooo!" screamed the vampire, releasing her immediately.

The two clowns arrived and flung the net. Which missed the Vampire Mayor, but neatly entangled Lancelot and Ben who were in the process of trying to get on their feet again.

Limping slightly, but slowed not one whit for it, the vampire charged at Barmy, possibly considering him to be the weakest link in a most peculiar chain. Barmy dropped his useless sword and with neither thought nor hesitation launched himself forward in a rugby tackle at the vampire's knees.

"Leave this to me!" Pendragon called bravely, stepping between them at the crucial moment. Barmy's arms wrapped round a pair of furry legs and the musty scent of old theatrical costumiers filled his nostrils as they both crashed to the ground.

"He's getting away!" shouted the clown Rowan as Vampire Mayor Brocklehurst broke out of the circle and began to run, with almost blinding speed for someone of his bulk.

"The net!" gasped Lancie. "Ben, the net!" They scrabbled free and grabbed the net between them, although by now the Vampire Mayor was out of reach.

"After him!" the tall clown shouted in Facecrusher's voice.

It was too late. It was all too late. Barmy scrambled to his feet in time to see the Vampire Mayor reach the corner of the stall.

Where the slim, green-clad figure of a handsome youth stepped out swinging a curious stone-ball weapon on a chain.

"Don't kill him, Aspen!" Lancie shouted. "We need to capture him alive!"

Barmy and Lauren both took off in furious pursuit, Barmy now half-mad with the excitement of the moment. Without so much as breaking stride, the Vampire Mayor veered away from Aspen and plunged down a narrow alley leading from the market square.

"After him!" called Rowan. "If we lose him now, we'll never find him.

But to Barmy's considerable surprise, the vampire emerged again almost at once, still running, but now pursued by a red and white spotted pantomine horse. He veered again to avoid Barmy and Lauren and ran directly into Lancelot and Ben, who threw the net.

This time it worked. The net fell like a dream, enveloping the Vampire Mayor completely. He tripped and fell headlong, then writhed and struggled, hurling abuse and entangling himself more tightly. Bodies piled on top of him in an untidy heap until he was totally subdued.

Barmy climbed out of the melee, panting. "I didn't think we'd make that," he said to no one in particular.

"Grrr," agreed the pantomime horse.

Chapter Twelve

"Right," said Lancelot Bong briskly once everyone had settled. "Where do we go from here?" He looked from one face to another, as if expecting a definitive answer.

"Presumably," Aspen said thoughtfully, "Mayor Brocklehurst will revert back to normal at sunrise. He might be prepared to cooperate with us then."

"The trouble is," Facecrusher put in, "sunrise might be too late."

"You don't think Tanaka will start his attack tonight do you, Facecrusher?" Pendragon asked in alarm. Facecrusher was looked on as the expert on Tanaka, having been silly enough to marry him some years before.

"No," Facecrusher said. "No, I don't. But everything's moving far faster than we anticipated. According to Lancie's information, my husband's plan was to smuggle in the vampires and leave them lying low until the attack occurred. Then they were to cut loose and sow confusion among the defenders. That was your information, wasn't it, Lancie?"

"Absolutely, dear lady," the Bong confirmed.

"And that hasn't happened," Lauren murmured.

"No, indeed, it hasn't," Facecrusher agreed. "We lost absolutely no time in getting back, but even so we arrived to find the vampires have already made a move. They've infected poor old Harry, who's now in the process of turning into one of them."

They turned to look at poor old Harry, who was incarcerated, like some overgrown canary that thought it was a bat, in a wicker cage hanging from a beam in Lancie Bong's main living room.

"I'll kill you!" poor old Harry screamed. "I'll rip your throats out! I'll eat your livers! I'll drink your blood!" He had been very abusive, on and off, since they shoved him in the cage, although the consensus was he should calm down by morning.

"And of course," put in the Amazing Presto, "poor old Harry's the only one we know about. There may be others."

"For all we know, they may already have infected the whole Keep Council and every officer in the Army," said Pendragon.

"I doubt that has happened," Facecrusher said soberly, "but it's close to the point I was making about tomorrow being too late. If they've bitten Harry already, who knows who they plan to bite tonight?"

"So the sooner we search out the crypt the better, what?"

"That would be my feeling," said Facecrusher carefully.

"It seems to me," Lauren said in that high, clear voice she adopted when she was taking charge, "that we cannot afford to work blind in this thing. The longer we take to find the vampires' crypt, the weaker our own position becomes. It seems obvious to me we must persuade Mayor Brocklehurst to tell us where he was when he got bitten and anything else he knows about Tanaka's vampires."

"I won't talk!" screamed the Vampire Mayor, shaking the bars of his wicker cage in such agitation that it began to swing like a pendulum. "You'll never make me talk! You won't hear me talk until hell freezes over!"

"I have a plan." Ben said suddenly.

"What's that, Ben?" asked Lancie.

"I'll beat him up," Ben said.

64

"I'll talk! I'll talk!" screamed the Vampire Mayor.

"Can I beat him up anyway, Lancie?" Ben asked, disappointed.

"You can't beat him up anyway, Ben. You can't beat him up at all, come to that. He may be a miserable vampire now, but try to remember he's really poor old Harry Brocklehurst and it's our duty to save him – if we can – and besides, he's agreed to talk."

"It's a trick," Ben muttered darkly. "Go on, Lancie, let me at him."

"Don't move, Ben," Lancie ordered. "Right, Harry, I'm glad your better self isn't completely buried. Now, where are Tanaka's vampires?"

"I'll talk," said the Vampire Mayor, "but only to you, Lancelot. Send the others away."

"It's definitely a trick," Ben said. "You just let me bash him. I'll get the truth out of him. And have some fun."

"You're a disgrace, Ben," Lauren said fondly.

"Don't you think it's a trick, Madam Obedniga?"

"I don't see how it can be – he's safely in the cage. What do you think, Lancie?"

"Only one way to find out," said Lancelot Bong briskly. "You lot trot off next door. Make yourselves some tea or something. I'll see what he's got to say. If he tells us where Tanaka's vampires are, well and good. If not, I can always let Ben at him afterwards."

"Goodie," Ben grinned.

"I'm not sure I like this," Barmy remarked as they trouped into the next room.

He went to brew tea from a blackened kettle bubbling by the hearth. Aspen came across, ostensibly to help him.

"Are you avoiding me?" she asked him quietly.

Barmy was so surprised he almost dropped the kettle. "No," he said quickly. "No, of course not. No, not at all." He felt a blush rising from his boots to flower like a

65

blossom in his cheeks. "Why should I – why do you think I'm avoiding – "

"You've hardly spoken two words to me since you came back from your own world," Aspen said. "Lauren's fine – we still get on great. But you – I don't know . . ." She shrugged. "I thought you liked me."

"I do. Oh yes, I do. Believe me, Aspen, I do. I like you a lot. A lot. Yes. Oh yes, you're not wrong there. Like you is what I certainly – oh good grief, I'm babbling. What I mean to say – "

"No, it's all right," Aspen said soberly. "I get the message. I hear what you are saying. So . . ."

"So?" asked Barmy, thoroughly confused.

"So that's all right then," Aspen said. She took a mug of brew in each hand and walked away. "Tea, Facecrusher? Tea, Presto?"

Barmy stared after her, convinced he had handled something badly, but not quite sure exactly what. Ben appeared at his elbow and followed his gaze. "I think Aspen is very attractive, don't you Barmy?"

"Yes," Barmy said truthfully. "Yes, I do."

"I think she has lovely elbows."

Barmy looked at him in bewilderment. Ben looked back blankly.

After a moment, Lancie Bong burst through the door in a state of high excitement. "He talked! He's told me everything!"

"Everything?" Facecrusher asked.

"Everything he knows," said the Bong. "Which isn't much, but it's enough. He doesn't know when Tanaka will attack, but he does know where his vampires have set up their crypt inside the Keep. Tally-ho!"

"Fantastic!" Facecrusher exclaimed in genuine delight. "What's the plan?"

"Collect up stakes and go get 'em!" Lancelot exclaimed.

"Bless 'em, bash 'em, hack 'em, slash 'em! I'll lead the way!" He grabbed a mug of tea from Aspen and in his excitement downed it in a single gulp. "Come on," he called. "Don't hang about!"

In the general bustle, Barmy found himself the only one who wasn't smiling. He had noticed two small red marks on the left-hand side of Lancie's neck and was trying very hard to remember if they had been there before.

Chapter Thirteen

They had arrived – thankfully no longer in disguise – in the old quarter of the town, an area characterized by narrow streets, tall and tatty overhanging buildings and a pervasive pong of sulphur and boiled cabbage.

"What on earth is that smell?" Lauren had asked loudly when they first encountered it.

"Cheap food and alchemy," the Amazing Presto exclaimed distastefully. "Most alchemists seem to drift to the old quarter until they turn lead into gold and can afford something better." He pointed. "Your Möbius Warp man, Kendar, used to live just down that street."

Lauren nodded, suitably impressed.

"Where are we going, Lancie?" Barmy asked eventually. He had decided to say nothing about the marks on the neck, which had in any case proved more like pimples than bites on closer inspection. It struck him as sensible simply to keep his eyes open and his wits about him. If the Bong started to behave strangely, he could always tell the others. If not, then he avoided making a complete idiot of himself.

"Fortress Armatrag," the Bong said briskly. "The original Keep, the very first ever built here."

"I didn't know there was a second fortress," Lauren said.

"Do you know exactly where the vampires are?" Aspen asked. She was walking up ahead with Lancelot, holding a lantern. Eynek, who disliked walking in shadow, had abandoned Rowan for the moment and padded immediately behind her like a giant herald of impending doom.

"No, not exactly," Lancelot told her. "Harry didn't tell me exactly."

"You should have let me at him, Lancie," Ben said in his thuggy voice. "I'd have got him to tell you exactly."

"Now, Ben, we've been through all that. You keep forgetting Harry's an old friend of mine. We sit together on the Council. He's not even a true vampire yet – he's just a poor old buffer who's been bitten. It could happen to any of us."

"It couldn't happen to me," Ben said. He grinned suddenly. "I'd run away."

"I can't imagine you running away from anything, Ben," Barmy said honestly.

"I don't like vampires," Ben told him seriously.

"So what's the plan when we get there?" Facecrusher asked. She was accustomed to leading and obviously felt a bit uncomfortable with Lancelot making all the running.

"We'll have to split up into groups," the Bong said.

Barmy felt a sudden stabbing of unease. It might not be all that easy to keep an eye on Lancie if everyone was splitting up. And even if he did spot anything peculiar, how was he going to tell the others if they were racing around at some far corner of the castle?

"What size groups?" Facecrusher asked.

"I don't know," the Bong said frowning. "I hadn't worked that out. Why do you ask, dear lady?"

"If we break into large groups, it will take us a very long time to search a building the size of Armatrag Keep. If we break into small groups, we might be in trouble with the vampires when we find them."

"Besides which," Pendragon said suddenly, "it's night now, which means the vampires won't be lying in their coffins waiting patiently to be staked. They'll be up and around, looking for people to fang."

"Grrr," Eynek said.

"He says he'll protect you, Draggie," Rowan translated.

"Oh, I'm not afraid for myself," Pendragon said loudly. "Not at all." He gave a modest little laugh. "I think I can take care of myself. I was only concerned for others."

"Good for you," Rowan grinned.

"All the same," Aspen said, "Pendragon has a point. Even if Mayor Brocklehurst has told us exactly where they have been hiding out, it's unlikely we'd find them there now."

"Yes, as you say, unlikely – what? But wherever they've gone – and I agree with Draggie they could have gone anywhere – they have to come back to their coffins."

"Why?" asked Lauren suddenly.

"Their coffins are lined with earth from their original graves," put in the Amazing Presto, who seemed to know a fearsome amount about vampires. "It's the only way they can get a good day's sleep. And, of course, without their sleep they simply wither away in a week or two. So Lancelot is right – they have to come back to their coffins sooner or later and they'll be anxious to make that sooner. Most vampires return every night, just before dawn."

"Ah yes, but – " said Pendragon forcefully, "if they're not in their coffins now, that means they're out and about. And if they're out and about, that means they're fanging people. And if they're fanging people, that means they're infecting people. And if they're infecting people, that means they are creating other vampires. And if they're creating other vampires, that means it's not much use us staking the ones in the coffins because the whole place will be full of the new vampires they infected." He looked around, smiling smugly.

"If we stake the originals, the rest get better!" Aspen sighed. "You are a twit, Draggie."

"Ah yes, but only if it hasn't gone too far."

"Well it hasn't, has it?" Aspen snorted.

They turned a corner and Barmy suddenly found himself staring up at the towering silhouette of one of the oddest buildings he had ever seen.

"Good grief!" Barmy breathed. "What is that?"

"We're here," the Bong said cheerfuly. "This is Armatrag Keep."

Chapter Fourteen

They went out, like the animals from Noah's Ark, two by two. Ben went with Lancie. Facecrusher joined forces with the Amazing Presto. Aspen, to Barmy's immense chagrin, paired off with Pendragon. There was no question of separating Eynek from Rowan, of course (and no means of doing it if there had been). Barmy, whose luck had run out months before, was stuck with his rotten little sister, Lauren. Each pair went equipped with one dozen sharpened wooden stakes and two leather-headed mallets. Each party member was further equipped with a Church Militant medallion, personally blessed by Lancie, and guaranteed – so he assured them – to bring good luck.

As a solution to the dilemma Facecrusher had raised, Lancelot Bong proposed that should any two-person party hit upon a vampire, they were to take no action on their own, but rather call for help, or otherwise make contact with one or more of the other parties. Nobody was to tackle a vampire unless they had it outnumbered by at least four to one.

It seemed a reasonable safeguard, although now he had actually entered Armatrag Keep, Barmy was beginning to wonder if it was enough. The place was as spooky as a House of Horrors.

Since the battery in Lauren's torch was running low, they were equipped with a more traditional light source – a wooden shaft with a head of twisted straw dipped in pitch. This torch spat and flared, creating the sort of pong a vampire could have smelled a kilometre away and casting eerie shadows which danced along beside them like an asylum chorus.

The Keep itself was a perfect example of the most bizarre architecture Barmy had seen in either of the two worlds he inhabited. It was built like a rabbit warren, with passages and tunnels leading into passages and tunnels, staircases descending into chambers that were little more than open pits, ladders giving access to chambers no larger than a linen cupboard, archways opening onto archways onto archways, and doors which led to dead-end galleries.

And everything, but everything, was ornately decorated with scrolls and whorls, fragments of bas-relief, murals, little gargoyle heads or abstract shapes. It was like walking through a baroque nightmare. It was also extremely confusing.

"Do you know how to get back to the entrance from here?" Barmy asked.

"Yes," Lauren said shortly. The smell of burning pitch gave her a headache, which had shortened her normally short temper even further.

He did not believe her, but knew better than to argue when she was in that mood.

There was a vague, aimless quality about their progress. The Bong's plan, such as it was, simply broke the party into smaller units, each one instructed to search diligently for Tanaka's vampires – or at least for Tanaka's vampires' crypt. Everyone had taken a different passage from the entrance; and that was that. There was no coordination, no signal system, no arrangement to meet up at some central spot, not even, now he came to think of it, any help in finding their way through the maze of passages.

And that was odd, for surely Lancie, as Keep Treasurer and Secretary, must have known where he could put his hands on plans of this old building. Barmy found himself wondering about those marks on Lancie's neck again. And because he had a vivid imagination, finely honed by D & D, a disturbing picture started forming in his mind.

Barmy coughed. "Did you notice two funny little marks on Lancie's neck, Lauren?" he asked. "Like . . . sort of, bites?"

"Don't be silly," Lauren said. Which seemed to put an end to that little conversation.

They reached a worn stone staircase which descended steeply into darkness.

"Shall we try down here?" Barmy asked.

Lauren stared down the stairs trying unsuccessfully to peer beyond the narrow pool of dancing light. "It's the sort of place vampires might like, isn't it?" she remarked uneasily.

"Yes. Are we going down?"

After a moment, Lauren said, "I suppose so."

There were so many better ways this whole operation might have been carried out. They could have started with a plan of Armatrag Keep.

And weaponry. Barmy was carrying a sword, which he already knew would be useless against a vampire unless he managed miraculously to cut its head off. Lauren was completely unarmed, so far as he knew, although she was now carrying the sack of sharpened stakes and the mallet. What way was that to equip a vampire-hunting party?

Barmy imagined how it might have been had Face-crusher been in charge of the operation. Everything would have run so smoothly. Why hadn't Lancie gone about it like that? *Because Lancie had been bitten*, a little voice told Barmy as he set foot on the first of the steep, worn steps. *Because Lancie is infected*, said the little voice. *Because Lancie is now three quarters vampire himself*, the little voice insisted. *Because Lancie has gone over to the bad guys!*

74

"Lauren . . .?" Barmy stopped on the stairs so abruptly that Lauren cannoned into him.

"Oh for heaven's sake, Barmy – don't do that!"

"I'm worried about Lancie," he told her bluntly.

"The bite marks?"

So she had been listening. "Yes. Did they look like bite marks to you? Did you notice them at all?"

"Yes, I noticed them," said Lauren who noticed everything. "And no, they didn't look like bite marks to me. They looked as if he'd cut himself shaving."

"Lauren," Barmy said with exaggerated patience, "Lancie has a beard."

She was opening her mouth to reply when suddenly there was pandemonium.

Chapter Fifteen

A resounding crash echoed from the darkness below, followed by a rush of footsteps similar in many respects to a cattle stampede; all headed up the stairs in the general direction of Barmy, who was standing three steps down with his mouth hanging open.

At the same time, a rush of chill air whooshed down the corridor as if an outside door had blown open. A howl of human pain echoed after it, reverberating horribly from one baroque wall to another.

And as if that were not enough, there emerged into the torchlight from another direction a boiling mass of rats in full, terrified flight, squeaking, stumbling, tripping and climbing over one another in panic.

Lauren screamed. "Rats!"

Barmy leaped back to avoid whatever was stampeding up from below and found himself standing ankle deep in rats. For a moment he froze, then he screamed too. The chill draught stopped abruptly, but a new sound filled the air, like the erratic beat of leather wings. Barmy drew his sword and attempted with no success at all to cut a swathe through the rats. He had horrified visions of the creatures swarming over him, but they seemed to be in too much of a hurry to do anything except flow past him like a stream in spate.

The leather wings belonged to bats. They appeared quite suddenly, pouring down the corridor like smoke, in the opposite direction to the rats, so that Barmy found himself standing at the confluence of two streams, one flowing in one direction at his feet, the other flowing in the opposite direction above his head. Below him, in the darkness of the stairwell, some other horror was approaching.

The howl of human pain was replaced by a series of heartrending groans, which seemed actually to be coming nearer. Although he had a lot on his mind, Barmy thought he had the sounds pinpointed in a branch corridor about eight metres from the staircase.

"Do something about these rats!" shrieked Lauren in the utterly unreasonable tones of someone accustomed to getting her own way.

There was something following the rats! Something large and, if the panic-stricken rats were anything to judge by, very, very dangerous. But Barmy had a more immediate concern. There were shapes rushing up towards him from the darkness of the stairwell.

A white figure emerged from the branch corridor, wailing. The rats flowed around it without a moment's hesitation in their flight. Behind them, a monstrous creature emerged from the darkness, hurtling down the passage like an express train. Barmy flung himself to one side only just in time, for the creature's hairy pelt actually brushed his cheek.

"Grrr," it acknowledged briefly as it careered past.

"Eye – " Lauren called, but obviously realized as she did so it was far too late.

"Wow . . . ow . . . owwwww . . ." wailed the white-robed figure in the manner of a ghost. Torchlight fell on its face to reveal the Amazing Presto. He was sucking two fingers of his right hand.

Overhead, the last of the bats disappeared down the corridor.

"Presto!" Lauren exclaimed. "What on earth are you . . ."

They were children! The creatures from the bottom of

the stairs were children! They were dressed in rags, their skin was black with grime and their hair was filthy and matted, but they were definitely children – almost a dozen of them staring up at Barmy with huge, brown, saucer eyes. Not one was more than seven years of age, judging by appearances. All carried sticks or clubs.

"Who are you?" Barmy asked, in something of relief.

" – doing here, Presto? Where's Facecrusher?"

"'Oo wants ter know?"

Presto shuddered. "Bats," he said. "I disturbed a colony of bats. I hate bats. Facecrusher went to explore one of the galleries."

The bats came from an entirely different direction, Barmy thought. Aloud, he said to the urchin who had spoken, "I do. My name is Barmy Jeffers."

"The bats came from a different direction," Lauren told Presto.

"That's a dumb name," said the urchin.

"That's as may be," Barmy said, "but this isn't a dumb sword." He waved it to impress the cheeky little twit.

"I dispelled them magically," said Presto with great dignity. "Unfortunately the principle of conservation of energy dictates that they appear somewhere else. Which they did; apparently quite close by."

"Conservation of Energy is a principle of physics," Lauren said, suddenly intrigued.

"I know."

"And it works in magic too?"

"Oh yes."

"That may not be a dumb sword," the urchin said to Barmy, "but there are twelve of us and we've got clubs."

"Why are you sucking your fingers, Presto?"

"Lauren, I think we've got a spot of bother here," Barmy said.

"I got them caught up in the door I opened to let out the bats."

"So if you don't step aside, Grotface, me and my mates will pound you to a pulp," the urchin said aggressively.

"Oh, you poor thing," Lauren said sympathetically, if somewhat uncharacteristically, to Presto.

"Lauren . . ." Barmy said. To his horror, he heard something else approaching, from behind him this time. But he dared not turn his head to look, convinced the urchins would attack the moment he took his eyes off them. The situation, he knew, was rapidly moving out of his control (while his stupid sister chatted blithely to his stupid colleague). The sword was an absolute bluff, of course: he would never use it against little children. But the little children all had clubs and – apparently – no such inhibitions.

"Here," said Lauren, "let me take a look – you may have cut yourself." She had always been fascinated by the sight of blood.

"Lauren!" Barmy hissed in desperation. He knew better than to attempt to call on Presto, who never involved himself in physical violence. Whatever was coming up behind was close now. He almost fancied he could feel its hot breath on the back of his neck.

The garrulous urchin suddenly took a step back down the stairs, eyes wide as saucers. "Here," it said, "I didn't bargain for that!"

"Now look – " Barmy began.

"You win, Grotface," said the urchin bluntly; and dropped his club.

"Grrr," said a voice behind Barmy's right ear; and a great head came over his shoulder to stare threateningly at the children.

Relief flooded through Barmy. Absently he reached up to scratch Eynek's ears. To the children he said firmly,

79

"This is Eynek, the world's most brutal and savage attacking dog. One word from me and he'll have you. Right, Eynek?"

"Grrr," Eynek agreed. Barmy glanced round in time to catch him rolling his eyes horribly.

"So you behave yourselves and do what you're told – is that understood?"

"Yes, Grotface," said the leading urchin meekly.

"Good heavens," Lauren said, having exhausted the topic of Presto's stupid fingers, "what have we here?" She came across. "Who are your smelly friends, Barmy?"

"Do I have to put up with this crud, Grotface?" the urchin asked Barmy stoically.

"Button your lip, kid!" snapped Lauren, who loathed small children like the plague. "You'll need to get yourself sluiced down before you join my little party."

"Hear that?" the urchin called across its shoulder. "Blondie wants us to clean up."

There was a ragged chorus of boos, interspersed with raspberries.

"Look here," Barmy said, taking charge manfully before the situation degenerated further, "you'd better tell me who you are and where you've come from." He pointed to the leading urchin. "You talk."

"We're orphans, Grotface. No names, no pack drill. From the Wilderness."

"From the Wilderness?" This was from the Amazing Presto, who had stopped moaning long enough to wander over since nobody was paying attention to his sore fingers any more.

"That's right. I like your robe – did you embroider all them little stars yourself?"

"Thank you," Presto said. "But no, I didn't. What were you – "

"What were you doing in the Wilderness?" Barmy asked loudly, determined to retain the initiative.

"We was living there. We was *born* there."

"And exactly who are you?" Barmy asked. "I mean, how do you come to be all together? Are you part of a family, or refugees from an orphanage or what?"

The group of children giggled. Even their leader smiled. "No orphanages in the Wilderness, Grotface. The Baron has better ways to spend his money. I suppose you could say we was family. We're the Skangdazzle Tribe." The smile broadened and a note of pride crept in. "We're probably the meanest little kids in the world." The smile vanished abruptly. "As you'd find out if you didn't have that elephant to protect you."

"Grrr," Eynek said.

"Never mind that," said Barmy, wondering suddenly where Rowan had got to. Eynek usually did not wander far from him. "What are you doing here, in Armatrag Keep?"

The urchin sniffed. "You think we like living in the Badlands? When there's an opportunity to get out of that place, you grab it. Right, Tribe?"

"Right!" chorused the Skangdazzle Tribe.

"What my brother means is how did you get here?" Lauren said coldly. "So why don't you cut the sarcasm and tell us that, little man?"

"I'm not a little man, I'm a little woman," said the urchin angrily. "We're all little women." She raised her left hand, fist clenched, and said, "Sisterhood!"

Eleven left hands came up in unison, fists clenched. "Sisterhood!" chanted the Skangdazzle Tribe.

Barmy groaned inwardly. "Just tell me," he said carefully, "how you got here."

"We heard Baron Tanaka's men planning to transport some vampires into the Keep – nobody takes any notice of little kids." She shrugged. "When we found out when the cart was leaving, we hitched a lift."

"With the vampires?" Barmy gaped.

"Sure, with the vampires. That's what I'm telling you!"

"Weren't you afraid?"

"Of what?" asked the urchin. "They're asleep all day."

"Do you see what this means?"

"No, Barney, not entirely," replied Lauren.

"If these girls came here with the vampires," Barmy said, "they know where we can find the vampire crypt!"

Chapter Sixteen

Presto returned with Facecrusher in a matter of minutes. Eynek took longer to find Rowan, but trotted back eventually with the little thief astride his shoulders.

"What's going on?" Rowan asked as he dismounted. He glanced without enthusiasm at the tightly grouped Skangdazzle Tribe. "Who are the brats?"

"Barmy thinks he may have found the way to the vampire crypt," said Facecrusher, who had been fully briefed before Rowan arrived. "These brats are going to lead us there."

"They're from the Badlands," Lauren said.

"Ever thought they might be spies?" asked Rowan bluntly.

Barmy, who hadn't, said rather foolishly, "What?"

"Spies," Rowan repeated. He examined the twelve grubby little girls with evident distaste. "Tanaka's known to use children as a fifth column. Nobody ever suspects them until it's too late."

"What do you think, Facecrusher?" Lauren asked, her voice suddenly wary.

Facecrusher shook her head slowly. "I doubt it. I've heard something of the Skangdazzle Tribe and they have no love for Tanaka, my husband. Of course there's no way of being sure. Rowan might be right."

They all turned to look at the Skangdazzles, who glared back silently. Eventually Facecrusher said, "Since we can't be sure and since we need them, I suggest we take it that they're not spies – at least not necessarily spies – but we keep a close eye on them. Fair enough?"

"Suits me, sister," said the garrulous urchin.

"I wasn't talking to you," Facecrusher said sourly.

They moved out shortly after that, the Skangdazzle Tribe in the lead, down the staircase that Barmy and Lauren had been set to explore before everything fell around their ears. It led into an open, stone-flagged chamber with a single, arched outlet. On the wall opposite was a massive painting of a grinning demon head, its open mouth large enough to swallow a grown man whole.

"This way," said the Tribe spokesperson, moving to the arch. Barmy found himself drawn to the demon head, which was a wonderful piece of nightmare art.

"Come on, Barney!" Lauren hissed, as the remainder of the party vanished through the archway.

"Yes, just a minute," Barmy said. The painting was not, he was sure, part of the original Keep. The style was too lifelike and plain, lacking the scrolls and whorls of the remaining ornamentation. And the colours were too bright, as if they had been painted only recently. He reached out to touch it and fell into the open mouth.

He was too surprised even to cry out. He pitched forward, dropped, lost his balance completely and sat down firmly on his bottom to find himself sliding through total blackness (his torch having been snuffed out) along some sort of chute. And just when it seemed the seat of his pants must go up in flames – or at very least rip apart to add to his embarrassment – he emerged into bright light, dropped perhaps another three metres straight down and landed, fairly softly, in a pile of straw.

"Strewth!" he exclaimed, as he picked himself up and dusted bits of straw from his clothing. He was in a plain stone chamber, illuminated by several torches in wall brackets, with a short flight of stone steps leading to a closed exit door in the wall opposite the heap of straw. Above him, in the stone-flagged ceiling, was the opening through which he had dropped. The chamber was empty, except for seven mahogany coffins in a row along the wall to his left.

"Strewth!" Barmy said again, fighting back the panic-stricken conviction that he had miraculously found the vampire crypt.

Maybe Rowan was right and the Skangdazzles were spies – or even tough young saboteurs bribed or beaten to do Tanaka's will. He found it hard to believe, although he could think of no real reason why it couldn't possibly be true. What did he know of the children? They had emerged from the darkness at the bottom of the staircase, called him Grotface and threatened mayhem until Eynek cooled them down. None of it was what you'd call a glowing testimonial.

On the other hand, spies were supposed to be incon-spicuous and friendly, so they could worm important information out of you. Spies didn't call you Grotface and threaten you with clubs. Or maybe they did.

The coffins had brass handles, highly polished. And his rotten sister Lauren was carrying the sharpened stakes.

Barmy looked across at the doorway, wondering if it might be locked. He had no reason to assume it was, except his luck. With his luck it would be locked, with the biggest, meanest vampire of the seven sleeping on the key. Except that it wouldn't be sleeping, would it? This was night-time. If there were vampires about, they would be up and around, climbing head first down walls, peering thirstily at beautiful young women in lacy nightgowns, backing away from crosses and so forth.

So that was all right then. Wasn't it?

Barmy found himself seized by an enormous reluctance to approach the nearest coffin, the lid of which – like those of the remaining coffins – was closed. He glanced back at the door again. Was it locked? Was it unlocked?

How many steps would it take him to reach it? Could he break it down by running at it with his head?

One of his feet placed itself before the other and he found himself that much closer to the coffin. Why hadn't he carried the stakes? He knew it was a mistake to let Lauren carry the stakes.

He fought down his panic and allowed his feet to carry him two steps closer to the coffin. Although the lid was closed, it was not sealed. It was not nailed down to keep the corpse from leaping out, or anything of that sort. In fact, it was not closed properly. It lay on top with a narrow slit along one side, just wide enough for fingers to reach down to draw aside the lid.

He found himself standing by the coffin, looking down on it, looking at that slit where the lid did not join and remembering a solo adventure gamebook he'd once read. In this gamebook he (playing the hero, a bloodthirsty individual named Pip) had found a sinister underground crypt, entirely lined in pink veined marble. There was a single coffin in the crypt and you had to solve a riddle to get into it. Barmy, who was good with riddles, got through the puzzle effortlessly and the coffin opened to reveal a rather friendly monster called the Poetic Fiend.

He wondered what the betting was that the monster in this coffin would be friendly. Before he could think any more, he reached down and flung back the lid, which crashed to the stone floor with a noise that would have wakened the dead.

The coffin was empty.

Empty! Barmy felt relief flood through him like a burst dam. No vampire. No animated skeleton. Not even a mouldy old corpse, rotting away quietly to itself. Nothing but an empty coffin with a bit of earth in the bottom and –

A bit of earth in the bottom? He'd found it! He'd found

the vampire crypt! It had to be. Vampires set up their crypt with a bit of grave earth in the bottom of their coffins so they could get a good day's rest. Who else would put earth in a coffin?

He turned to the next coffin in line. If there was earth there, that would confirm it.

If there was a vampire there, that too would confirm it, a small voice whispered in his head.

Barmy walked to the second coffin, wondering if he was brave, mad or just thick, and threw back the lid. When he found that coffin too was empty, he realized he had been holding his breath and released it explosively. The interior was lined in pale blue satin . . . and sprinkled with earth!

Well, well. Barmy stopped and looked around, his mind racing. So the Skangdazzle Tribe might be in Tanaka's service after all. Certainly they had said nothing about the demon face and the shaft, although they must certainly have known about it. All very suspicious. But he had found the crypt now and that was the main thing. The question was, what to do about it?

With growing certainty, he opened up the next two coffins, finding them, like the first, empty but for grave earth. Tanaka's seven vampires were obviously on the prowl, heaven only knew where. But they would have to return here before dawn. That was their weak spot. That was their Achilles heel, as Barmy's history teacher liked to say. They would have to return and when they did –

When they did, what? At the moment, if the seven vampires returned, it would be to find a nice defenceless little snack awaiting them without so much as a stake in his back pocket. He threw back the next two lids.

What he needed to do, Barmy thought, was to make contact with the others. Bring them back here, stakes and mallets at the ready, to lay an ambush for the vampires.

In that sort of surprise attack, they wouldn't stand a chance, even if they all arrived back together, which was unlikely in itself. He almost felt sorry for the monsters. He threw back the last coffin lid and froze.

The Reverend Lancelot Bong was lying in the coffin, face deathly pale, hands crossed on his chest, eyeteeth grown so long that they protruded over his lower lip like monstrous yellow fangs.

Chapter Seventeen

The Bong's eyes opened suddenly and his hands shot out. Barmy ran. He careered up the short flight of steps to the door as if the devil himself were in pursuit. He flung open the do – He flung ope – He flung –

The door was locked! It would have to be, of course! He'd never had a moment's luck since he stumbled into this stupid world. Locked solid, probably chained and bolted too for all he knew, with no way out. He glanced over his shoulder in time to see the Bong rise from his coffin like all four horsemen of the Apocalypse. He was wearing a long, black Dracula cape over the familiar plate armour.

"What?" asked the Bong drearily, like someone in a deep trance. His eyes were unfocused and he moved with a sort of horrid deliberation that was somehow more terrifying than speed could ever be.

Barmy took the entire set of steps in a single bound and raced across the chamber. He had some small hope of jumping high enough to reach the shaft through which he had fallen, smaller hope still of climbing back up its steep and slippery surface. But small though these hopes were, they remained the only hopes he had.

"What?" asked the Bong again, in that dreadful hollow voice.

Barmy screeched to a halt. There was something rising up out of the heap of straw!

"Help!" whispered Barmy. He wondered how he had got himself into this mess. He wondered why he had walked through Lauren's Möbius Warp instead of staying tucked up warm in bed. Then he remembered what had happened while he was lying tucked up warm in bed and put such philosophical speculations out of his head.

"What?" repeated Lancie Bong a third time, rather more firmly now.

The thing in the heap did not rise up very far. Hands attached to the muscular arms began to tug at the straw to reveal a short, broad and terribly familiar figure. It was Ben!

"Was it you that fell on my head, Barmy?" Ben asked crossly. "You knocked me out." He rummaged in the straw and withdrew his ornate crossbow.

"Ben! Lancie's been bitten! He's turned into a vampire!"

"What?" asked the Bong in something far more like his old familiar tones. "What? No, don't worry, Barmy – this is just another of my incredibly cunning plans."

Barmy turned in time to see his old friend remove the yellow fangs and drop them into a pocket of his cloak. Lancelot grinned broadly. "Bought them in a joke shop. Good, aren't they?"

"You're not . . .?"

"What? A vampire? Not yet anyway. Bless 'em, bash 'em, hack 'em, slash 'em's still my motto. Tally-ho and all that, what?"

It sounded like the old Lancie. "He's not a vampire, is he, Ben?"

"I never thought so, Barmy," Ben said.

"'Course I'm not a vampire, Barmy. Feel." He stuck out his hand.

Barmy took it cautiously and found it warm.

"See?" said Lancie Bong. "Hot blood."

"But what are those marks on your neck?" Barmy asked. "Like bite marks."

"Bite marks," said the Bong. "I got eaten by a

mosquito when we were trying to find you and Rowan on Tarantulus's island."

The tension started to drain out of Barmy's stomach. "This may sound a silly question, but what were you doing lying in a coffin wearing false fangs and a vampire cloak?"

"Sleeping," grinned the Bong. "Ben and I had this plan when we found the crypt. Ben was going to hide in the straw with his crossbow while I pretended to be a fellow vampire to lull their suspicions when they came back at dawn. Except it was a very comfortable coffin and I fell asleep."

"And you fell on my head and knocked me out, Barmy," said Ben.

"But," Barmy said, "that isn't what you were supposed to do if you found the crypt. You were supposed to call in the others so you outnumbered – "

"No fun in that," said the Bong.

Barmy shook his head helplessly. The Reverend Bong was a natural anarchist, even when he was the one to make the rules. Eventually Barmy said, "How did you get in here?"

"Through the door."

"It's locked."

"No, it isn't, Barmy," Ben said. "You were turning the handle the wrong way." He moved towards the steps, presumably to demonstrate, when there was a small but definite noise outside. Barmy froze. "What's that?"

"They're coming back!" the Bong said. "Tally-ho!" He jammed his false fangs back in and leaped into the coffin.

"He means the vampires are coming back, Barmy," Ben said, lest Barmy had missed the import of the situation. "They must have finished ripping people's throats out." He actually smiled. "This is very good, Barmy. It means we can try out Lancie's plan."

"What am I supposed to do?" Barmy hissed. "I don't even have a stake."

"You can have one of mine, Barmy," Ben said. "I don't mind that because you're my friend."

"How many do you have?"

"Seventy-four," said Ben who obviously did not believe in taking chances.

"You hide in the straw with Ben," Lancie called from the coffin. "As soon as they come in, I'll sit up and engage them in conversation. While they are suitably distracted, Ben will shoot them with his crossbow and you can stake them afterwards to make sure they stay dead."

"But Ben," Barmy protested, "crossbow bolts won't damage vampires!"

"These ones will," said Ben. "They're made of wood."

The sounds outside were definitely coming nearer, and there was no question of a single vampire either. To judge by the racket they were making, all seven were on the way – and drunk.

Ben pulled Barmy down and covered him with straw, before burrowing deep into the heap himself. From his place of concealment, Barmy had a clear view of the door.

"Here," Ben whispered.

Barmy felt a bundle of sharpened stakes being pressed into his hand. "Thanks," he whispered back.

"Good luck!" called the Bong cheerfully from inside his coffin.

They lapsed into silence and waited.

From his vantage point deep within the straw, Barmy watched the handle of the door. The noise outside stopped abruptly and for a long time there was total silence. He was just beginning to wonder if the vampires had wandered off somewhere (or worse, become suspicious) when the handle on the door started turning.

Barmy watched, hypnotized. Time seemed to have slowed down alarmingly so that the movement continued, fraction by fraction, for an eternity. His grip tightened involuntarily on the bunch of stakes. Then suddenly the door was open and a horde of figures swarmed into the chamber.

"Wooooo!" exclaimed a hollow voice, which Barmy only just recognized as that of Lancie, even now rising like Lazarus from the comfort of his coffin. It was an impressive sight, even to Barmy who knew what was going on. The Bong had drawn his lips back to reveal the totality of those hideous false teeth and spread his arms, so the black cloak looked like batwings. He came up stiffly, from the waist, in a single flowing movement. "Wooooo!" he said again, having evidently decided this was the standard greeting between vampires.

Beside Barmy, Ben started to rise, his crossbow at the ready.

It was going wrong. Barmy knew it was going wrong. He had known it was going wrong almost from the instant the door opened. There were too many people. Even if all seven vampires had returned at once, there were too many people. And most of those people were too small for the coffins. Too many and too small. And besides, one of those who just loped down the steps was Eynek!

Barmy heard the bolt of Ben's crossbow click back and hurled himself sideways on to his lethal little friend. "No, Ben!" he screamed. "Don't shoot! Don't shoot!"

"Woooo!" Lancie said again, never able to resist the urge to overact.

"It's one of them!" a high-pitched voice called. "It's a great smelly ugly vampire!"

Out of the corner of his eye, Barmy saw the entire Skangdazzle Tribe fall upon the hapless Lancie with their wooden clubs.

93

Chapter Eighteen

It took him half an hour to sort out that little lot. Much of the time was spent bandaging the Bong and nearly ten minutes went into persuading Ben to talk to him again. The whole mess had one positive aspect, however: it put paid to Lancie's leadership potential. By the time Barmy had finished, the Church Militant's finest flower looked much like an armoured mummy.

"Well," he said fatalistically, "somebody else will have to look after things from here, what? You'll have to number me among the walking wounded."

In the end, Facecrusher thankfully stepped forward to take charge.

"Right," she said briskly. "First priority is to have Aspen and Pendragon join us. We've located the crypt now, so there's no need for them to be wandering around getting into trouble. Besides, if all the vampires return at one time, we'll need every hand we can get." She drew herself up. "A volunteer to find them?"

She looked around the sea of raised hands and one raised ear. "Right," she said again. "I think Eynek is probably best equipped to bring them back since he can follow scent. Will you go with him, Rowan?"

"OK," Rowan said.

"Get them here as quickly as you can. On my reckoning we've still got an hour or more before dawn, but there's no guarantee the vampires won't come back earlier, so we'd better be prepared."

"We're on our way," said Rowan briskly. "We'll have

them back before you've properly noticed we're gone. Right, Eynek?"

"Grrr," said Eynek, loping to the door.

Facecrusher's preparations were a lot more thorough than Lancie Bong's had been, although there was one area where she agreed with him entirely. "I think the notion of hiding in that pile of straw was excellent," she said. "Will you go back there, Ben?"

"Only if you tell Barmy to stop knocking me down," Ben said.

"Stop knocking Ben down, Barmy," Facecrusher grinned. "And I think you'd better hide in there with him." She looked around the chamber. "Presto, can you levitate into that shaft Barmy fell down?"

The Amazing Presto nodded.

"How good's your attack magic against vampires?" Facecrusher asked.

Presto shrugged. "Not very. Unless, of course, I call a slith."

"I don't think that will be necessary," Facecrusher said quickly. "You just stay up there out of harm's way. Now Lancelot, I'm not sure you should be taking part in these proceedings at all . . ."

"Nonsense, dear lady: a little bruising, that's all. A little stiffness. A little loss of blood. A few broken bones here and there. A cracked skull. A partially amputated leg. A – "

"Yes, I thought so," Facecrusher said, "you're beginning to rave again. Presto, can you levitate Lancie into the shaft with you and hold him there comfortably until he recovers from the shock?"

"No problem," Presto said.

"Now you Skangdazzles," Facecrusher went on. "You're small enough to hide behind the coffins, which is what I want you to do. When you're in place, hold still and keep quiet and don't attack anything until I give the signal. Now listen carefully, everybody: this is the plan. For the moment, I'll keep watch outside, but when Rowan comes back, he'll take over that job and give us early warning when any of the vampires return. Pendragon, Aspen and Lauren will be concealed within earshot in one of the side corridors. So will Eynek. I propose to wait openly in this chamber as bait. Any vampire or vampires who come in will find me here examining a coffin as if I've just discovered the crypt. Hopefully they will assume I am alone and helpless, at which point they will naturally attack. While their attention is diverted, Pendragon, Aspen, Rowan and Eynek will undertake a flanking movement to make sure that when the fighting starts no vampire gets away. Those of us in here, meanwhile, will stage a mass attack. Even if all seven of them come back at once, I don't think they will stand a chance."

"That's a good plan, Facecrusher!" Ben beamed benevolently. For some reason he liked hearing plans, whatever their nature.

"Thank you, Ben. Now, let's share out the stakes, then places, everyone."

As the stakes were being passed around, Lauren said, "What happens if the vampires come back before the rest of our party?"

"In that case, wait until they're all into the chamber, then attack. You and I, Lauren, will just have to make sure none of them escapes."

But in the event, Lauren need not have worried. Less than eight minutes later Rowan rode Eynek down the corridor followed by Aspen and Pendragon, who looked as if they had been quarrelling about something. Facecrusher went over the final plan once more. "Any questions?" she asked when she had finished.

It was Lauren who spoke up again. "Just one," she

said. "When we've dealt with the vampires, what are we going to do about the Baron?"

There was a long moment's silence. Presto, who had not yet levitated himself and Lancie up the shaft, said, "She's right, Facecrusher. All this is just a holding operation. Tanaka's the real problem."

"That and the canaries," remarked the Bong, who seemed to have been slightly concussed during the Skangdazzle attack.

Presto ignored him. "You take my point, Facecrusher? He's managed to get seven vampires into the Keep. No matter how well we deal with them, it doesn't solve anything. He'll just send in seven more. Or fourteen more. Or a hundred more. Or if he doesn't use vampires, he'll try something else."

"I take your point, Presto," Facecrusher said soberly. "In fact, I've been ahead of it for some time. So far as I'm concerned, the vampires are only our immediate worry. None of us are ever going to rest easy in our beds until my husband is safely under lock and key." She hesitated only marginally. "Or dead."

"I think we should kill him," Ben said flatly. "You can always get a divorce, Facecrusher." He frowned. "Although if we kill him, you won't need to, will you?"

Facecrusher pursed her lips. "There are two possible places he might be since Barmy wrecked his castle. One is the Pileggi Mountains. The other is a very nasty area they call the Valley of Doom. But before we can do anything about the Baron, we have to get his vampires out of the way, otherwise the entire Keep will be overrun. So if there are no more questions . . ."

There weren't. Everyone took their places and waited.

And waited.

"Barmy . . .?"

"Yes, Ben?" Barmy whispered from his burrow in the straw.

"I hope I don't lose my nerve when the vampires arrive, Barmy."

"Why would you do that, Ben?"

"Because vampires make me very nervous," Ben said. "I don't worry about ghouls or wights or lyches or anything of that sort, but vampires make me very nervous."

"Vampires make everbody very nervous," Barmy told him.

"Do they, Barmy? Do they really?"

"Yes, really," Barmy said. "You'll be all right."

"I hope so, Barmy."

They waited.

And waited.

With no means of telling the exact time, it seemed like an eternity to Barmy before the door of the chamber opened again. But it was Rowan who came down the steps, not any vampire.

"It's long past dawn, Facecrusher," he said simply.

Facecrusher, who had been squatting immobile on a portable stool in the middle of the floor, stood up frowning fiercely. "Yes, I know." She glanced around and called. "You can come down now." To Rowan she said, "I knew it was past daybreak, but I didn't want to admit it to myself."

Barmy stood up gratefully and brushed straw from his clothing. "What's happened, Facecrusher?"

"We've been sold a pup," Facecrusher said.

"Grrr?" said Eynek, who had followed Rowan in.

"It's a figure of speech, Eynek," Facecrusher said tiredly. "What I mean to say is that this crypt must be a decoy – something to divert our attention."

"We saw the vampires moving their coffins in here, sister," said one of the emerging Skangdazzles earnestly.

"I believe you," Facecrusher told her simply. "But the real crypt must be somewhere else. It has to be. Once the sun rises, no vampire can survive outside its coffin. And since they're not here, they must be somewhere else."

"Simple logic," Lauren said, entering through the door. Aspen and Pendragon were close behind her.

"So what's the new plan, Facecrusher?" Ben asked. He looked relieved.

"The new plan is we start to search again," Facecrusher said. "The vampires must have gone back to their crypt somewhere and at least it'll be a lot safer for us to search during daylight since they'll be asleep. It's messy, but it's not a disaster." She looked around, then walked over to the shaft through which Barmy had fallen. "Lancelot, Presto – you can come down now."

But there was no reply. Barmy, who was standing close by, took a torch from a wall bracket and angled it so he could see up the shaft. There was no one there.

Chapter Nineteen

The ransom note arrived just twelve hours later – twelve hours in which they had no success at all in locating the real crypt of Tanaka's vampires. It was addressed to the Keep Council and intercepted by Facecrusher in the absence of the Mayor (who remained firmly locked in his wicker cage, dozing most of the time, but waking occasionally to call for revolting snacks of raw liver and uncooked tripe). She called an emergency meeting of the adventure party, most of whom were trying to catch up on a little sleep, and handed round the scrap of yellow parchment without comment.

When it was passed to Barmy, he found it covered in large, somewhat spidery handwriting, saying:

Curse you all. You have caused me sufficient aggravation to last a lifetime, but now it's over. I have your rotten Secretary and Treasurer, the Reverend Lancelot Bong, not to mention that cretin of a wizard, the so-called Amazing Presto.

For the moment they are safe, although a little bruised since I am amusing myself by throwing rocks at them. But unless you deliver over to me the Sceptre of Saul I shall have them killed very slowly within sight of the walls of your pestilential Keep.

If you want to see your friends alive, leave the Sceptre by the Twisted Rock and I'll have it collected. If not, I'll do them in and feed any bits left over to my vampires.

You have until noon tomorrow to make up your

*minds. Only one person is to come to Twisted Rock with
the Sceptre. No tricks or I will kill them anyway.*

Hoping this finds you as it leaves me,
Yours faithfully,
Tanaka Bt.

"What's the Sceptre of Saul?" Barmy asked. For some
reason the sight of Tanaka's handwriting had left him
even more uneasy than the content of the note. It
reminded him of the horrid reality of the man – the
bloated body, the hideous features, the animal teeth.

"It's a sort of ceremonial mace kept in the Town Hall,"
said Aspen. She frowned. "I wonder why he wants it."

"Maybe he's found the way to make it work," suggested
Rowan.

"What does that mean?" Aspen asked.

"Haven't you heard the legend of Saul's Sceptre?"
Pendragon exclaimed in the sort of tones that implied he
must be talking to an idiot.

"Probably not," put in Lauren coldly, "but doubtless
you will tell her shortly."

Pendragon, who was utterly immune to subtlety, said
expansively, "The Sceptre once belonged to Saul the
Ranger, who was probably the mightiest warrior the world
has ever known." He hesitated, as if a sudden thought
had struck him, then added, "In his day". He leaned
forward, his features contorted in a look of dramatic
sobriety. "They say it was the Sceptre that made his
reputation. It was supposed to be the ultimate weapon. It
was supposed to call down thunderbolts which would melt
any armour ever made or smash through stone walls three
metres thick."

"Grrr," breathed Eynek, who was easily impressed.

"The Sceptre was made by a great wizard, or possibly
the gods themselves. It was given to Saul in appreciation

101

of his honesty, decency, upright nature and striking good looks. But he was the only one who had the secret of its use."

"And nobody ever got it to work?" asked Aspen. "Throw thunderbolts and so forth?"

Pendragon shook his head.

"Maybe it was all a myth," suggested Lauren thoughtfully.

"Saul the Ranger was no myth!" exclaimed Pendragon as if he had been offered a personal insult. "He was a shining example of goodness and truth and – "

Facecrusher coughed. "No doubt. But I didn't call you here to discuss a dead hero. We need to decide what to do about this note."

"I think that's a matter for the Council," Pendragon said, obviously miffed at being interrupted.

"The Council took six months to decide whether they should paint the inside gate green or blue," Facecrusher told him bluntly. "If we leave it to them, they'll still be arguing about the agenda when my husband is slaughtering our friends. If there is going to be action on this, we have to take it." She looked around soberly. "Agreed?"

"I'm not at all sure – " Pendragon began pompously.

"Shut up, Draggie," Aspen said.

"So we're agreed on that," Facecrusher said. "Good. Now can we agree on what we propose to do?"

"I'd give him the stupid Sceptre," Aspen said promptly.

"You'd give him Saul's – " spluttered Pendragon, who seemed to have talked himself into a personal interest.

"Isn't that a bit . . . well, dangerous?" Barmy asked, surprised to find himself in agreement with Pendragon for once. "You know," Barmy continued. "Thunderbolts and things."

"It hasn't thrown a thunderbolt for centuries," Aspen said. "If it ever did. Even if you believe the legend, it never threw a thunderbolt for anybody except Saul – isn't that what you just said, Draggie?"

"Yes," Pendragon admitted.

Although he disliked arguing with Aspen, Barmy felt compelled to say, "If Rowan isn't right and Tanaka doesn't know how to make it throw thunderbolts, what's he want it for?"

Aspen shrugged. "It's valuable, for one thing. In fact, as an historical artifact it's probably priceless. Tanaka's greedy. I imagine that could be reason enough."

"There may be another possibility," Lauren put in suddenly. "He may want it as a symbol – a sort of rallying point for his forces when he attacks the Keep. We know he plans to attack the Keep, remember. He may feel if he has the Sceptre, it would be good for the morale of his army."

"That's right," said Pendragon eagerly. "Saul had an incredible number of loyal followers, followers who would die for him, and the Sceptre was their rallying point. If Tanaka – "

"I'd still give it to him," Aspen said.

"You'd still – ?" Pendragon exploded. "I suppose you think somebody like Tanaka would take it and say thank you very much and just give back Lancie and Presto? I suppose you – "

Facecrusher waved him into silence. "Why would you give it to him, Aspen?" she asked quietly.

"Because it's bait," Aspen said. She shifted her position. "Draggie's right – Tanaka won't release Presto or Lancie whatever ransom we pay. He'll hold them until he has what he wants, then he'll kill them and send us back the bodies. So we've no option but to try to mount a rescue – but the only problem is we don't know where to mount it. Tanaka could be holding them anywhere."

103

"Facecrusher thinks she knows where they are!" Pendragon said angrily.

Aspen sighed. "Facecrusher thinks they might be in the Pileggi Mountains or the Valley of Doom. They might be. Even if she's right, we don't know which one. Even if we knew which one, we don't know exactly where. It would take us weeks to search the Valley of Doom thoroughly – if we survived. It could take us months to find an army in the Pileggis, let alone two hostages. We don't have that sort of time: Tanaka is threatening to kill them at noon tomorrow."

"So what's your solution, Aspen?" Facecrusher asked.

"Yes," Ben nodded. "What's your plan?"

"My plan is to do exactly what he's told us to do. Get the Sceptre and leave it at Twisted Rock. But it won't be just one person – we'll all go. And we'll stay concealed and watch and follow whoever collects the Sceptre right back to where Tanaka's hiding."

"That's a good plan, Aspen," Ben said.

"Yes," Facecrusher nodded thoughtfully, "I think it is. What do the rest of you feel?"

"I don't think we – " Pendragon began.

"So it's agreed," said Facecrusher firmly. "Excellent. I think we should move as quickly as we can. There is one point we need to sort out though – "

"What's that, Facecrusher?" Ben asked.

"This is only going to work if we lull my husband into a sense of false security. Obviously we have to pretend to comply with the ransom demand. We have to get the Sceptre and we have to appear to send only one person to Twisted Rock and those of us who follow have to be very well concealed and careful. All that's fine. But Tanaka will still be suspicious – that's his nature and that's what's kept him alive so long. So we have to go further."

"How do you mean – further?" Aspen asked.

"It's important we select the right person to take the Sceptre. We need somebody who looks innocent and a bit helpless and nervous. Somebody who doesn't look much of a threat. Somebody not very big or muscular. Somebody you wouldn't think of as being dangerous or clever."

Barmy suddenly found everybody had turned to look at him.

Chapter Twenty

Barmy felt as though he had been walking for days. Saul's Sceptre, slung across his right shoulder with a few cucumber sandwiches tied to it in a red spotted handkerchief, grew a little heavier with every step. To make matters worse, the day was arid and hot, the ground beneath his feet rough and barren as a desert.

He was, moreover, feeling nervous. Twisted Rock was in the Badlands south of the Keep: Tanaka's country, an area where wolves were only the smallest of your problems and you were quite likely to walk into anything from a werebear to a giant weasel. In theory, of course, the others should have been following close behind.

But like so many original arrangements, this one had gone for a burton the minute the situation moved out of theory into practice. And it was his own sister who had torpedoed it. She reckoned Tanaka must have posted men (or monsters) to keep a lookout from the very minute the Sceptre left the Keep.

There was no way the rest of the party could stay concealed and so it was agreed that Barmy should actually set out alone as Tanaka had instructed, and the others would creep out later and catch him up.

Now, alone in the Wilderness, he was having second thoughts. Even if Tanaka left him alone, he was still liable to be attacked by anything – animals, reptiles, monsters, anything – and there was no chance of help. None. None at all. Small consolation that the others would follow sometime.

He was not very happy with his sketch map either. It

was a joint effort between Ben and Pendragon, both of whom claimed to know the area well. But they had argued about it solidly for three quarters of an hour and on one occasion actually came to blows and had to be separated by Facecrusher. In the end they produced a compromise.

Now he was unhappy that this was his only guide. What if Ben had been right and Pendragon wrong? What if Pendragon had been right and Ben wrong? All a compromise map did was make sure they were both wrong.

He knew he would find Twisted Rock, as it was a prominent landmark, visible for quite some distance. But he was worried he wouldn't reach it in time. He was working to a deadline. They were all working to a deadline. Without the Sceptre, Lancie Bong and the Amazing Presto would be hacked to bits at twelve noon precisely. Barmy had started out at dawn, but it was now, by his best estimate, ten o'clock. He should have reached the Twisted Rock nearly an hour ago. And he felt as if he had been walking forever.

Where was the Rock? And where, he wondered, were his companions? Had they even left the Keep yet? If so, had they managed to stay hidden from Tanaka's spies?

Despite his sense of urgency he stopped to place his back against a boulder and rest his feet for a moment. He was considering the advisability of removing his boots for a moment when he saw the snake.

It was not a large snake, not a monstrous snake, but it was the first snake he had ever come across in this world: a creature half a metre long and brightly patterned as a tropical fish. It was perhaps two metres away and slithering slowly towards him with a peculiar gleam in its beady little orange eyes.

"Grr," something growled almost in his ear.

For one glorious instant he thought it must be Eynek.

Then he looked around and found himself staring into a pair of yellow eyes. It was not Eynek. It was not even a dog, but some sort of sabre-toothed cat about the size of a leopard. Barmy stopped dead. In a moment of irony almost too bitter to be borne, he noticed beyond the cat a broad sweep of lava apron out of which rose a great rock in the shape of a howling dinosaur.

"Grrrr," growled the sabre-tooth again, a low, ominous rumble that, on reflection, did not sound a bit like Eynek's friendly greeting.

"Hisssss!"

Barmy risked a backwards glance and saw the snake had rounded the boulder too and was still heading towards him. It was not moving very fast. All the same, he thought he could outrun the snake.

He wondered if it was possible to outrun a leopard.

"Nice kitty!" Barmy murmured soothingly. The big cat made a darting run towards him, then stopped. Barmy decided to keep his mouth shut.

Vaguely he remembered reading somewhere that if you stood absolutely still and didn't sweat too much most predators ignored you unless they were hungry. It helped that he was half-paralysed with fright already.

Of course, if he stood still, it would give the snake time to catch up with him.

"Hissss!"

"Grrrr!"

Barmy decided he'd been reading far too much and ran. Out of the corner of his eye, he saw the snake skitter away in alarm at the sudden movement. The sabre-tooth, however, was bounding after him.

He was heading for Twisted Rock with some lunatic notion that he might climb it and escape the cat. But even that unlikely idea depended on his reaching the Rock first – or even reaching it at all. A glance over his shoulder suggested he might be better off banking that the sabre-tooth was struck down by a meteor. It was gaining on him with alarming rapidity.

Barmy reached the edge of the lava apron and turned. The cat stopped too, regarding him cautiously. It looked neither nervous nor frightened, merely dreadfully efficient and supremely confident. The yellow eyes suggested it was going to kill him, not out of hunger or malice, but simply because he was there.

Twisted Rock was only a few hundred metres away. Two or three minutes' walk at the most. Was that close enough? If the big cat killed him – as almost certainly it would – would Tanaka's men have the wit to search around a bit when the Sceptre was not propped against the Rock as arranged? Would they find this poor shredded corpse?

The cat sprang, possibly encouraged by the maudlin expression on his face. Barmy suddenly realized he had been feeling so sorry for himself that he had not even bothered to unsheath his sword. In an attempt to avoid the charge, he stepped backwards, caught his heel on the edge of the lava apron and sat down heavily. He could not have timed it better if he tried. The cat sailed over his head with a puzzled expression on its face.

He was lucky once, but it was unlikely he would be again. He scrambled hurriedly to his feet to find the cat had already turned and was launching a second charge. There was no time to draw his sword now. Barmy crouched and swung the only thing to hand – Saul's Sceptre, with the spotted handkerchief and cucumber sandwiches still attached.

Suddenly, everything seemed to be happening in slow motion. He watched the rippling muscles of the great cat's body as it arched gracefully towards him. He felt his legs straighten as he moved to meet the leap. He saw the

Sceptre glinting in the sunlight as it swung like a long metallic club towards the beast . . .

The head of the Sceptre made contact with the sabre-tooth and instantly the great beast vanished!

Barmy turned completely round, carried by the momentum of his blow. There had been no thud, no crunch, no jarring of his arm – apparently no impact. But the sabre-tooth cat was no longer there. He looked around him in bewilderment. There was no cover nearby, nowhere that the cat could hide. Yet it was no longer there.

He was still trying to figure out what on earth had happened when he noticed that the head of Saul's Sceptre had begun to glow with a pale, unearthly light.

Chapter Twenty-One

The glow faded even as he watched, leaving the Sceptre inert as before. He looked around again, more carefully this time, but the sabre-tooth had definitely disappeared. There had to be a connection. For the briefest instant, the Sceptre of Saul had become active. But why?

What was it Pendragon had said? Only the noblest soul, the purest heart, the most honest mind could activate the Sceptre? That ruled Barmy out right away.

But what then had turned it on?

An unpleasant thought was creeping into his mind. Supposing – just supposing – it wasn't the user who decided when the Sceptre worked at all. Supposing it was the time it was used. Supposing whatever force resided in the Sceptre was cyclical – it came and went like the tide.

So supposing the energy in the Sceptre really did come and go, maybe over a period of years or even centuries . . . and supposing Baron Tanaka knew the Sceptre was about to become active again.

It would explain an awful lot. It would explain why the Baron had decided to move against the Keep at precisely this time. It would explain why Lancelot Bong learned about the vampires so easily. It would explain the phoney crypt, which was in such an obvious place that Barmy had literally fallen into it. What he was looking at was a set-up, a clever trap designed to take the Reverend Bong hostage. In all probability, the Amazing Presto got caught up in it accidentally: the one Tanaka was really after was the Bong, whose position as Keep Secretary and Treasurer made him an important man.

And it had all worked out exactly as Tanaka planned. The Bong was kidnapped. The Mayor, as an unexpected bonus, was quietly turning into a raving vampire. And Barmy was blithely delivering up the Sceptre to Tanaka as instructed.

If the Sceptre was indeed becoming active and if only half the stories told about it were true, it would make Tanaka the most powerful man in the country – probably the most powerful man in the world!

And here was Barmy delivering it!

The shadow of the great Rock fell upon him. Close up, it looked more like a howling dinosaur than ever and did absolutely nothing for his mood. But what to do? If he left the Sceptre at Twisted Rock as instructed, he risked giving Tanaka the key to world power. If he didn't, Lancie Bong and Presto would get their throats cut at noon.

He was on his own with the most terrifyingly difficult decision of his entire life. What should he do?

He stared at the Sceptre, now inert as it was the moment he had first set hands on it. Had he imagined the glow? It had only lasted a second or two that he had noticed. But whatever about the glow, he certainly had not imagined the cat. And the cat had disappeared.

What should he do?

There was a sound behind the Rock.

The sabre-tooth? Had the sabre-tooth simply run off? Was it even now creeping back on him from behind Twisted Rock? This time Barmy drew his sword. He set the Sceptre down, leaning it against the base of the Rock, and moved forward cautiously to find the source of the sound.

He was four steps further on when the ghouls jumped him.

Barmy had a lot of experience with ghouls, since the

repulsive creatures made up the bulk of Tanaka's followers and army. The two who landed on him from behind were typical of the breed: tall, but painfully thin and consequently very light. He twisted instinctively, so suddenly and so strongly that he broke free at once. As he turned to face them, he knew at once these were Tanaka's creatures. Each carried a short sword. Wild ghouls tended to avoid the use of weapons, apart, of course, from their natural fangs. And they tended to avoid fights as well, unless they outnumbered their opponents by a substantial margin.

Barmy lunged. The nearest ghoul parried and the fight was on.

After a sweaty five minutes during which Barmy felt like something out of a swashbuckling pirate movie, a suspicion began to dawn on him that whatever else they might be doing, the two ghouls were definitely not trying to kill him.

After a moment more, the suspicion was dramatically confirmed. Barmy had been leaping from one lava outcrop to another like a demented goat when he leaped once too often and caught his foot in a shallow fissure. He teetered for an eternity, arms flailing, then lost his balance and crashed down on to his back with such force that the sword flew out of his hand.

One of the ghastly creatures hurled itself on top of him. Barmy twisted violently, convinced he was in the process of being eaten, this being a ghoul speciality. But no fangs met his flesh and he realized almost at once the creature was attempting to pin him to the ground. And might well have succeeded, light though it was, had not the second ghoul joined in. At some point during the ensuing tangle, Barmy wriggled free. He jumped to his feet no worse for wear, but somewhat disorientated, and looked round for his sword.

It had fallen some distance away. Before he could make a move towards it, one of the ghouls grabbed his ankle. Barmy kicked out violently to free himself and had the satisfaction of hearing the ghoul howl. The hand let go of his ankle and he was off like a jack rabbit, heading for the sword.

But the second ghoul was on its feet and moved with sufficient speed to insinuate itself between Barmy and his weapon, waving its own sword threateningly. Barmy screeched to a halt and turned. His plan, such as it was, was to circle the Rock and pick up his sword from the opposite direction. Ghouls were fundamentally thick and he was fairly sure this one would simply lope after him rather than make a real effort to cut him off again. He put on a fearsome burst of speed, careered around the base of the Rock and found himself racing towards a horde of nearly fifty ghouls approaching from the south.

Barmy screeched to a halt again, unmindful of the single ghoul pursuing him. What to do now? There was no way he could even think of tackling fifty ghouls single handed.

Or was there? What if the Sceptre really was active? What if its time had come and it switched on automatically when its user needed it?

The single ghoul pursuing fell upon his back. As the creature crashed upon the ground, Barmy bounded for the Sceptre propped against the Rock.

At once there was a massive howl of protest from the approaching ghouls, as if they somehow divined a danger to themselves. Although it might have been no more than an instictive reaction to his movement, the sound heartened Barmy. Maybe the ghouls knew more than he did. Maybe they feared the Sceptre.

But the small burst of optimism was his last. Before he could reach the artifact, the second ghoul he had been fighting appeared around Twisted Rock from the other direction and without a moment's hesitation snatched the Sceptre and ran.

For the barest instant, Barmy hesitated, then hurled himself after the creature. But as he turned the corner of the Rock, he ran full tilt into another ghoul party approaching from the west. It was only half as big as the horde from the south, but there were still more than enough ghouls to bury him.

Which they did with ghoulish glee.

Chapter Twenty-Two

Barmy came to with a small, but enthusiastic group of invisible gnomish blacksmiths pounding on his head with hammers. When he realized they were not going to go away, he opened one eye to the dim light of a prison cell.

It was a truly ghastly place: a filthy, stone-flagged chamber, tastefully furnished with a thin heap of rotted straw in one corner and the dried remains of something even worse in another. There was no window, although the top half of the studded door was composed entirely of metal bars, allowing sight of a narrow corridor through which dim light filtered.

He started to stand up and fell down again. He had a vague recollection of ghouls piling on to him like some demented rugby scrum, but after that matters were fuzzy to the point of blankness. The Sceptre was gone, of course, but so too were his sword and breastplate. There was some bruising on his arm, more on his right leg, particularly around the knee. His left cheek was tender, just below the eye, and his nose felt as if it might be flatter than it normally was. He suspected he looked a bit of a mess.

Keeping his back against the wall, he managed slowly to stand up without falling down again. There was no doubt in his mind that he was Tanaka's prisoner, although why the ghouls hadn't simply slaughtered him was beyond his understanding. Although it could happen yet. The cell might be the ghoulish version of a deep freeze. He shivered. It was cold enough.

How long had he been here? The only thing he had to

go on was his bruises, which had reached the stage of ripeness to suggest he might have been unconscious several hours.

He took a cautious step forward, swayed alarmingly, but retained his feet. He took another and, against all odds, felt a little better. The pounding in his head was fierce, but he seemed to steady a little.

Tanaka had the Sceptre! Barmy wondered if he had been right in his guess that the wonderful artifact became active at longish intervals. If this was the case, Tanaka could have started on the road to world mastery by now.

Was there a possibility that he might escape? The door was certain to be guarded. If he was going to get out, he had to use his head.

A tunnel! He needed an implement.

Looking around, nothing jumped out as a hot possibility. Or even a lukewarm possibility come to that. He quickly searched through his pockets, but discovered the ghouls had taken absolutely everything he possessed.

Although it was the last thing he wanted, his mind turned towards the heap of straw. This was not a new cell. In fact, it was a very old cell indeed, judging by appearances. Which meant he was not its first unwilling guest, not by a long chalk.

He started to search the straw.

It was a rotten job. The cell was damp and the straw had turned black and slimy underneath the surface. Furthermore, half a million crawling insects had marched in at some stage and staked out their claims. And the further down he went, the worse it became.

He took a deep breath, walked across and started on the other corner. The only thing buried there proved to be a dead rat, squashed flat and partially mummified. So much for his bright idea of tunnelling.

117

Barmy went back to the spot where he had woken up and sat down again.

After a minute, it occurred to him that the question wasn't what would they have done, but what did they do? Of all the prisoners who had been locked in this cell, surely at least one was as desperate as he was . . . and had the means to do something about it?

Barmy began to search again, starting with the stone-flagged floor. Sure enough, one of the flagstones seemed a little loose. He started to work at it until at last his fingers slipped into the crack. For a moment he was convinced he would not move it, then, quite suddenly, it came up all of a rush.

There was a narrow tunnel underneath.

He stared down into the hole, hardly believing it. But it was there, scraped out of the earth by some long dead prisoner. Without further ado, he lowered himself in.

The tunnel dropped sheer for about two metres, then levelled off, heading in what he took to be a northerly direction for a number of metres, then broke through into what looked like a natural cleft. Where the tunnel had been cramped and dark, the cleft was faintly illuminated by some form of phosphorescence which gave him just enough light to see. He squeezed along carefully and, after a few moments, found himself in a small cave.

He caught his breath as he stepped in. A dried out skeleton was lying on the floor. But otherwise the cave was empty. Barmy searched very carefully indeed, but the result remained the same. The cave was a dead end. He searched one more time, still without result, then made his way back.

He had one nasty moment when he found himself stuck, but he wriggled free eventually and pulled himself up, back into the cell. Out of some lunatic urge to keep things tidy, he pushed the flagstone back in place. At once it occurred to him that he was being stupid. If he could not dig his way out, he might use the tunnel as a hiding place and fool his captors that he had disappeared. Obviously he was the first to have discovered the tunnel (except for the skeleton, of course) since it had not been filled in.

He made to lift the flagstone again and found it jammed solid. He scrabbled at it until his fingertips were sore, but it made no difference whatsoever. In a moment of agonized frustration, he ran across and shook the bars of his cell. The door swung open easily.

Chapter Twenty-Three

He was in a deserted, ruined building, the cell he had occupied being one of the few parts of it still standing comparatively intact. For half an hour or so, he wandered through rubble-strewn corridors, occasionally stepping through broken walls and continuously worrying about the possibility of the roof caving in on him – at least in those areas where any roof remained. Why the ghouls had dumped him there he did not know.

Eventually he emerged from the building and discovered why the ghouls had dumped him there. He was overshadowed by a towering cliff-face, black and sheer. Around him was a line of ancient ruins, gripped by writhing twists of roots and other gnarled vegetation. Behind him, to the west, lay a densely-packed wall of matted fern and giant trees, strongly suggestive of a swamp. Before him, strewn across a rocky gradient which formed the valley floor, lay the bleached bones and rusting armour of scores – even hundreds – of warriors, as if some great battle had occurred here at some time. Except that by the remains of their insignia, the warriors all appeared to have been fighting on the same side . . .

Something had killed those warriors. Something *big*.

How long had he been unconscious? Had Tanaka got the Sceptre? Were the Reverend Bong and the Amazing Presto still alive, or had they already been slaughtered? Nothing that came into his head cheered him very much, but all of it prompted him to action. He walked at once to the battlefield and searched. He could not find what he was looking for – a sword which was still usable – but he did come across a wicked-looking battle-axe which was not too far gone with rust. Indeed, after he had cleaned it up a bit, it seemed a serviceable enough weapon. Now, where to go?

It was obvious he was in some sort of valley. The steep cliffs to the north looked quite impossible to climb, while to reach a second cliff-face far to the south could take hours and would probably leave him no better off. He did not fancy the swampland to the west, which left him only the one remaining alternative. He struck out eastwards, trying to ignore the skeletons.

As he did so, something crashed from the swampland behind him.

Barmy swung around, axe at the ready, then froze in utter terror. The thing bearing down on him was twice the size of an elephant, but there the resemblance ended. It was some sort of gigantic lizard, armoured with blue-green glistening scales and like nothing he had ever seen before. The body was gross, ending in a broad, scaly tail which enabled it to balance on hind legs thick as tree trunks. Its neck and head, by contrast, were almost delicate; the neck slim and tapering, the head something like that of a serpent and small in proportion to the body. It had slim forelegs, a little like arms, and short, stubby batwings protruding from its shoulders. Those wings were far too short for flying and must have represented an evolutionary degeneration from some time in the distant past when the species – whatever it was – could take to the air.

The ground shook as the creature lumbered towards him. It moved with astonishing speed for something of that size and bulk, eating up the ground between them at a truly alarming rate. He wondered if it was some sort of dinosaur, left over from the general extinction, then remembered that in this reality there might not have been a general extinction.

The thing was coming at him like an express train and he was standing philosophizing about the state of ruins. He had to do something; and he had to do it fast. The only thing to think about was what.

One of the craziest thoughts of his entire life occurred to him then. He remembered reading somewhere that most wild animals were afraid of humans at some level. And almost all wild animals were afraid of anything that exhibited erratic behaviour. Putting those two facts together . . .

Oh no, Barmy thought. But the conclusion was almost inescapable. Assuming he had the courage to carry it out. He took a deep breath. It was not so much courage as desperation. If he stood where he was, he would be eaten. If he ran away, he would be eaten. Therefore . . .

With a wild whoop, Barmy launched himself towards the dinosaur, brandishing his war axe above his head. "Bless 'em, bash 'em, hack 'em, slash 'em!" he yelled in lunatic imitation of the Reverend Bong. "Back off, you great flat-footed twit!"

To his absolute astonishment, the creature halted. So, naturally enough, did Barmy, since had he continued to run, he would quickly have come within striking distance, which would have meant having to fight the thing, which did not bear thinking about. He bent down and picked up a rock about the size of a hen's egg and hurled it at the beast. He managed a hit, since he could hardly miss a target that size at close range. The rock bounced off the heavy scales. The monster's head went up and it began a furious trumpeting, loud enough to rival the massed brass bands of several regiments. It began to thresh about wildly, braying and roaring, then plunged sideways before spinning on its own axis. All in all, the reaction seemed a bit over the top for such a small rock. Then he noticed something protruding from the dinosaur's right eye.

The creature was now hurling itself about with such abandon that he could not see properly what it was. Then the brute lurched forward and the great head swept past no more than a few metres away. It had been shot through the eye with a crossbow bolt.

He felt a tug at his sleeve. "I think we should retreat now, Barmy," a familiar voice suggested. "I don't think we can kill it, even with your big axe, however many times I shoot it."

The creature convulsed violently, gave vent to an earth-shaking roar, then keeled over with a mind-bending crash.

"On the other hand, I could be wrong."

"Ben!" Barmy exclaimed, open-mouthed. "You did it! You killed a dinosaur! You're absolutely incredible!"

"I'm not the one who ran at it with a hatchet," Ben said. He seemed a bit overwhelmed by what had happened.

"How did you find me?" Barmy asked. "What happened anyway? The last thing I remember was the ghouls jumping me."

"We followed you," Ben said. "At least Aspen and me followed you. The rest went after the Sceptre of Saul so they could rescue Lancie and Amazing."

"Where's Aspen?" Barmy asked at once.

"We split up to look for you."

"Will she be all right?" Barmy frowned.

Ben grinned. "Don't be silly, Barmy."

As they walked to the head of the valley where Ben had agreed to meet up with Aspen, Barmy said, "I don't suppose you know what's happened to Lancie and the Amazing Presto, do you? Or what happened to the Sceptre?"

"No," Ben said. Then added, "Yes."

"What?" asked Barmy.

"No I don't know what's happened to Lancie and Amazing, Barmy," Ben said. "Yes I do know what happened to the Sceptre."

"What? *What?* Come on, Ben!" Barmy exclaimed impatiently.

"They took it to Tanaka, Barmy," Ben said.

"Yes, yes, I thought they would," Barmy said quickly. "What I meant was, do you know where Tanaka has it?"

"In his new fortress, Barmy. The one you didn't demolish with a slith. It's at the end of the Valley of Doom," Ben told him.

Barmy took a deep breath. "And where is the Valley of Doom?" he asked patiently.

"We have just left it," Ben said.

Chapter Twenty-Four

"We have problems," Aspen said gravely. They had met up at the head of the valley and even her pleasure at seeing Barmy safe could not mask the worry on her face.

"What sort of problems, Aspen?" Ben asked.

"I cut across some high ground while I was looking for Barmy," Aspen explained, "and it gave me a view of the others – Facecrusher, Lauren, Rowan, Eynek and Pendragon. They've been ambushed."

"Killed?" asked Barmy quickly, a chill erupting from his stomach.

But she shook her head. "Captured. All except Eynek, who managed to run off. We should have known Tanaka would suspect we'd follow you. It was a fairly obvious move after all. I should have realized something was wrong when he sent a whole contingent of ghouls to attack you, Barmy. He wouldn't have needed so many if he thought the only thing we were going to do was leave the Sceptre quietly at the Rock."

"What happened?" Ben asked quietly.

"You know the arrangement," Aspen told him. "They were to keep out of sight and keep out of trouble – follow at a safe distance. And they did – that's the awful thing. Barmy, you wouldn't know about this, but the group of ghouls who captured you actually split in half. One half disappeared into the Valley of Doom with you and came out alone a little while later. The other half took the Sceptre. Ben and I said we'd see if we could find you. The others were to keep on the track of the Sceptre since that would lead us to Lancie and Presto – "

"It's more important than that," Barmy put in. "I think the Sceptre is starting to work again, the way it did for Saul the Ranger. It would be a dreadful weapon in Tanaka's hands."

Aspen blinked at him. "There's no good news, is there?" She shrugged. "Well, that only makes things all the more urgent. Our party was well behind, well out of sight when a second group of ghouls jumped them. There must have been more than a hundred, so they didn't stand a chance. Tanaka obviously planned the whole thing very carefully."

"So we're the only ones remaining free?"

She nodded.

Barmy closed his eyes. "So what do we do now?"

"Why don't we go and bash Tanaka?" Ben suggested.

"Ben's right in principle, of course. If anything's going to be done here, we're the only ones left to do it."

"Where did the ghouls take them?" Barmy asked.

"Come over here . . ." She led them to an area of high ground and pointed.

"What?" asked Barmy. All he could see in the distance was a clump of squat rocks.

"Tanaka's hideout," Aspen said.

"All I can see is some rocks."

"That's all there is to see. It's underneath them – some sort of bunker. You could walk past it a thousand times and never suspect. And since it's so close to the Valley of Doom, you don't get many people walking past it anyway. So – " she shrugged.

"Is it guarded?" Barmy asked. "Do you know?"

"No guards up top," Aspen said. "Presumably that's part of the camouflage. I imagine there are guards once you get underneath, though. There would have to be."

"Do you know the way in?"

"Only roughly," Aspen said. "I saw where the ghouls

126

disappeared with Facecrusher and the others, so I know the general area. I don't know if that will be enough to get us in, though."

"I know a way in," Ben said brightly.

They both turned to look at him in surprise. "Do you, Ben?" Aspen said gently.

Barmy asked, "How?"

"That's an old trog-warren," Ben said. "I had cousins there."

After a moment, Barmy asked, "What's a trog-warren?" Then, on second thoughts, "What's a trog?"

"They're a race of little people like Ben, except they live underground," Aspen said. "Very few people have ever seen them."

"I've seen them," Ben said. "I have quite a few cousins who are trogs. There used to be a whole tribe in that warren, but they moved on a few years ago."

"They're nomads," Aspen explained.

"So you think Tanaka discovered the warren and took it over?" Barmy asked.

"He must have," Ben said. "That's the entrance." He began to look sly. "Or rather, that's *one* entrance."

"And you know the others, Ben?" Aspen asked. There was a hint of excitement in her voice.

"I know all the others, Aspen," Ben said smugly. "I can get us anywhere inside you want to go."

"What are we waiting for?" Aspen asked.

Ben had led them to the nearest concealed entrance – which was, in fact, quite distant from the rocks where Tanaka's ghouls had disappeared. They entered a realm of beautifully constructed granite, limestone and marble halls, joined by broad stepped corridors and terraces, all brightly lit by luminescent globes which reminded Barmy irresistibly of electric bulbs, but obviously worked on some entirely different – and utterly mysterious – principle.

"It looks empty," Aspen murmured.

"We're on the outer edges, Aspen," Ben said. "Tanaka has probably only taken over the bit of the warren around the Throne Room."

"Which we have to get to," muttered Aspen grimly. "The only problem being how to do it without alerting the guards and getting ourselves killed."

"You leave that to me, Aspen," Ben said.

Two empty chambers further on, he stopped them with a gesture, knelt down and raised a concealed trapdoor in the floor. Steps led downwards into gloom. Ben turned to grin broadly at them. "I told you I knew all about this warren, didn't I? Used to play hide and seek down here, I did."

"When was that, Ben?" Barmy asked. Somehow he had difficulty imagining Ben as a child.

"Last year," Ben said.

They followed him downwards. Barmy had expected darkness, but these corridors had the same glow-globes as those above, except that here they were so dim it was like fumbling through a starlit forest.

"These are the cellars," Ben said, unmindful of the fact that even the topmost storey was deep underground. "The trogs kept their cider here to mature."

They must have drunk an awful lot of cider, Barmy thought, looking round him. The galleries seemed to stretch for miles.

"They drank an awful lot of cider," Ben remarked. He pushed open a wooden door. "I don't know what the Baron might keep here."

Barmy stepped through after him and found the answer in a chilling instant. There were seven coffins in the

128

chamber, identical in every way to those he had seen in Armatrag Keep.

But this time he somehow did not think they would be empty.

Chapter Twenty-Five

"You look and see what's in the coffins, Barmy," Ben said. "I'll stay here near the door."

Barmy swallowed hard. He was almost as nervous of vampires as Ben seemed to be. But before he could do anything, Aspen said quietly, "Let's not rush in without thinking. It's still daylight outside, so if this is a vampire crypt, they'll all be asleep in the coffins."

"So Barmy will be quite safe when he opens them," Ben said. Then he added thoughtfully, "And I'll be quite safe near the door."

"The only thing is," said Aspen, "did anybody think to bring wooden stakes?"

Barmy's heart sank. Vampires had been the last thing on his mind when he set out with the Sceptre. "I'm afraid I didn't . . ."

Aspen shook her head. "Neither did I. So – "

"I did," Ben said, grinning. "I always carry a supply of stakes in case I meet up with a vampire, Aspen."

Barmy's eyes flickered over the coffins. "Have you more than seven, Ben?"

"Oh, yes," Ben said. "A lot more. And two mallets." He blinked. "You can't be too careful, Barmy."

"We'll do this together," Aspen said. "You take the three closest, Barmy. I'll do the other four."

"And I'll watch the door," Ben said quickly.

"It'll be a bit scary, but it should be safe," Aspen said. "Even if they manage to wake up, they can't do anything until the sun sets."

Barmy nodded nervously. The last thing he needed was

a job staking vampires. But if the creatures were here, it had to be done. Besides which, if he backed out now, he would be losing face in front of Aspen. He took three stakes and a mallet from Ben and walked quickly to the nearest coffin so he would have no time to think. He closed his eyes for a second, took a deep breath to steady himself, then pushed back the lid.

There was a vampire inside, a tall, saturnine individual neatly dressed in a dark suit and black cloak, with telltale eyeteeth protruding well below its bottom lip. It was asleep, hands folded on chest.

Barmy hesitated. As veteran of a hundred horror movies, he knew the next bit was going to be absolutely awful, with the thing opening its eyes at the last minute and blood-curdling screams and spurts of –

Before his imagination could run riot, he placed the pointed end of the stake against the vampire's ribs and bashed it with his mallet.

The vampire fell into a pile of dust. As, oddly enough, did the stake.

"Hey, look at – " Barmy started to call to Aspen, then stopped, realizing she must have found out for herself since she was already opening up her second coffin. He moved on to his next coffin, feeling considerably more cheerful.

The vampire in the next coffin was a woman. She wore the diaphanous, low-cut, white flimsy nightgown thing female vampires always seem to wear in the movies and looked stunningly beautiful in a dark, slightly sinister way.

The movie heroes always hesitated at this point, smitten by such instant attraction that they fiddled around until the thing woke up and had them by the throat.

Barmy hesitated. "This one's a woman," he said to no one in particular.

"Kill it!" Aspen snapped. She was starting on her fourth coffin.

"Yes," Ben said from the doorway. "You just kill it, Barmy."

He placed the point of the stake over the heart and the woman's eyes flickered open. They were green, liquid pools that caught him like the eyes of a snake hypnotizing a sparrow. "Hello, handsome," she said throatily. Barmy's hand began to shake.

"Oh for heaven's sake!" Aspen leaned over the coffin and struck the stake sharply with her mallet. Both stake and vampire fell to dust. "What on earth are you playing at, Barmy?" Aspen asked, glaring at him angrily.

"I'm sorry," Barmy mumbled, reddening.

"Then do your other coffin and let's get on," said Aspen.

Barmy moved shamefacedly to his final coffin and pushed back the lid. For an instant he was seized by déjà vu. Lancelot Bong was lying in the coffin, wrapped in an opera cloak, his face distorted by those ludicrous false fangs.

"Lancie!" Barmy exclaimed delightedly. "Hey Aspen, Ben — I've just found Lancie!" He reached down and shook his shoulder. "Wake up, Lancie — we've come to rescue you." The Bong's eyes flickered open instantly. "Take out those stupid teeth," Barmy grinned. "You don't need the disguise any more." He tugged at the fangs. They remained immobile as real teeth.

"It's not a disguise," a soft voice said behind him.

Barmy swung round. Looming in the doorway was exactly the same vampire that had attacked him through his bedroom window, the one he had pushed off the wall with the handle of a broom. It was, without a doubt, the biggest, ugliest, most threatening creature he had ever seen.

Ben took off without a word. He bombed past Barmy and Aspen to disappear through the archway at the far end of the chamber.

"So we meet again, Barmy Jeffers," the creature said. "On my home ground this time."

"You know this thing?" Aspen asked in amazement.

"It's the one Tanaka sent to get me in my world," Barmy explained.

"What's it doing up before sunset?"

"Oh, we can move about quite freely any time of the day or night, just so long as we stay out of bright light," the vampire said. "You were lucky with the others – you just happened to catch them asleep and worked fast. If you'd been a little slower, or made a little more noise, or come in a little later, they'd have caught you. Right, Reverend Bong?"

"Right, Draccie," said a hollow voice behind Barmy. He swung round again to find Lancie climbing from his coffin, eyes glazed and staring.

"As I said," remarked the vampire at the door, "the teeth are not false. The Reverend Bong is one of us now."

"Let's get him!" Aspen yelled, launching herself towards the vampire.

Startled out of his shock, Barmy made to follow, but was seized from behind by steely hands. "Curse 'em, crunch 'em, fang 'em, munch 'em!" hissed the Bong in a ghastly parody of the Church Militant war cry.

Aspen swung her famous stone-ball weapon, aiming at the vampire's head. The creature reached out casually with one hand and caught the weapon, jerking it from her hand. "You think you can harm me with this?" he growled. He placed the ball of the weapon between his two hands and began to squeeze. "I shall crush this toy as easily as an elephant might crush an ant!"

133

"Just let me at your throat, Barmy," the Vampire Bong whispered. "I haven't had a decent snack in days."

Barmy slammed his heel down violently on Lancelot Bong's instep.

"Yipes!" yelped the Bong, releasing him at once.

"I shall crush – " said the vampire by the door again. He seemed to be having trouble crushing the stone ball. Sweat began to form on his forehead and a vein stood out at his temple.

Barmy twisted away. "You keep away from me, Lancie," he warned. "I don't want to hurt you, but I will if I have to and I've still got this stake." He waved it and the mallet, so that Lancie blanched.

"I shall cr – "

Aspen darted forward and kicked him on the kneecap, so that he teetered backwards and dropped the stone ball still uncrushed.

"You wouldn't use a stake on me, Barmy," said the Vampire Bong.

Which, Barmy thought with a sinking feeling, was probably correct. How could he bring himself to stake Lancie?

"Barmy!"

The thing by the door was running towards Aspen. Barmy launched himself forward without a second's hesitation, holding the last stake in front of him like a talisman. The Vampire Bong stuck out a foot and tripped him neatly, so that he stumbled a few paces before crashing to the ground. The other vampire tripped over his head and fell heavily. Aspen ran forward and karate kicked it on the ear.

But the thing only shook its head, rolled to its feet and dived on the prostrate Barmy.

Barmy felt the breath explode from his body and saw a dance of coloured lights before his eyes. He could smell the vampire's foetid breath. Powerful hands gripped his shoulders. Fangs sought his throat.

Barmy struck upwards with the wooden stake, using it like a dagger. For a moment he thought he had missed. Then a flicker of stunned surprise crossed the vampire's features and Barmy suddenly found himself smothered in a cloud of dust.

"You got him!" Aspen screamed excitedly. "You did it, Barmy! You got him!"

"Aaaargh!" gurgled the Vampire Bong, who seemed to be having some sort of fit, probably triggered by all the excitement. He writhed and threshed in the middle of the room, as if working himself to the peak of fury before deciding which of them he was going to attack.

Ben appeared at the arch through which he had disappeared, still running full tilt. He careered into the chamber, eyes wide. "We got trouble, Aspen, Barmy!" he gasped as he screeched to a halt beside them.

Chapter Twenty-Six

"What?" asked the Bong briskly. "What? What? What?"

"Tanaka," said Ben breathlessly. "On his way. Ghouls. Knows we're here."

"How are we going to get out of this mess?" Aspen asked grimly of no one in particular.

Barmy swung round in anticipation of an attack by the Vampire Bong, only to discover his teeth were shrinking visibly.

"Same as always," said the Bong, apparently in answer to Aspen. "We bless 'em, bash 'em, hack 'em, slash 'em – what?"

"Are you all right, Lancie?" Barmy asked cautiously. It was possible the Reverend Bong had been infected by one of the vampires they had just staked, in which case he would be undergoing a spontaneous recovery.

"I doubt if bless 'em-bash 'em-hack 'em is the answer this time . . ." Aspen said.

"Never felt better in my life!" the Bong told Barmy. "Touch anaemic, but I'll take iron tablets."

"Hello, Lancie," Ben said. "I see they've rescued you again." He had recovered his breath and was speaking in his old slow rhythm. "What's happened to Amazing?"

From somewhere beyond the arch through which Ben had entered, there filtered the sound of marching men. Or ghouls . . .

"Blessed if I know," said the Bong. "I'm a bit confused about what happened after that thing bit me."

"Are we going to stand here all day socializing, or do you plan to do something?" Aspen asked waspishly.

"I think Ben had the right idea a moment ago," Barmy said.

"We should run?" asked Aspen.

Barmy nodded. The marching steps were nearer now. Much nearer.

"Come on!" Aspen called and swung towards the other door. Which, unfortunately, was framing a seething mass of white shapes. "Too late!" she muttered, moving to scoop up her weapon on the floor.

The chamber was filling with Tanaka's ghouls. Barmy pulled the war axe from his belt and dropped into a fighting crouch. Ben had already unslung his ornate crossbow when the Bong did a very strange thing. Drawing himself up to his full height, he walked unarmed towards the ghouls.

"What kept you?" he demanded sharply. He swirled the long, black vampire cloak around him and Barmy noticed with a secret surge of excitement he had popped his false fangs back in. "These people are my prisoners. I have to take them outside on the Baron's orders. Stand aside."

He walked forward without hesitation and the ghouls parted like the bow-wave of a ship. "Prisoners – follow!" the Bong ordered over his shoulder.

Barmy looked at Aspen. Aspen looked at Barmy. They both shrugged and fell in behind the Bong. Ben released the tension on his crossbow and followed. Around them, the ghouls seemed restless and uncertain, but they kept their distance. Barmy found himself starting to count the steps he took. One . . . two . . . three . . . Still the ghouls held back, their faces masks of uncertainty and confusion. Four . . . five . . . six . . . They were going to make it! Seven . . . eight . . . Incredibly, they were going to make it!

They had almost reached the door when a soft voice

from behind them said, "Nice try, Your Holiness, but the charade is over now."

Barmy swung round and felt his heart drop to his boots. Dominating the chamber was the vast bulk of the Baron Tanaka, piggy little dark eyes glinting, bloodless lips drawn back in a chilling smile. He was surrounded by more armed ghouls than Barmy could count and he carried Saul's Sceptre in the crook of his left arm.

Both Ben and Aspen moved so quickly that Barmy had no time to draw breath.

"Eeeeeaghhhh!" screamed Aspen in a bloodcurdling yell and kicked the nearest ghoul so violently that it collapsed unconscious.

Ben had his crossbow loaded, fired, reloaded before the ghouls could make a move. He had aimed directly at Tanaka.

Tanaka raised the Sceptre and suddenly it was as if the whole scene had changed to slow motion in a movie. He could see the ripple of the muscles in Aspen's arm and back as she swung her weapon round and round.

The bolt left Ben's crossbow, quivering like a leaf in a gale, and followed a leisurely course towards Tanaka's throat. Tanaka himself was smiling still, as if unaware of the danger.

There was a sudden small flaring of light from the Sceptre, more a glow than a flash, and the bolt in flight vanished as if it had never been. Even in slow motion it was sudden. One moment the missile was there, the next it was gone.

Time reverted to normal. Aspen launched herself forward and cut a swathe through the ghouls with the spinning stone ball. Ben fired a second bolt which blinked out of existence exactly like the first. Barmy struck out with his war axe and had the satisfaction of seeing one ghoul reel away. Then a bright flash and a clap of thunder filled the chamber, bringing the fight to a halt before it had properly begun.

Barmy swung round again. The Baron was holding the Sceptre high above his head and now his entire body was glowing with a pale blue aura shot through with rivulets and streams of pure electric fire. Tiny lightning bolts licked out from the Sceptre, leaping and crackling, while the air filled with the smell of ozone.

"All right, you grot-faced little maggots!" screamed Tanaka. "Lay down your weapons or I shall blast you to oblivion!"

It stopped even Aspen. Slowly they set down their weapons. As they did so, the fire surrounding Tanaka faded. "That's better," he said softly. "That's much better." He gave a small signal and ghouls flooded forward to bind their hands and drag them over to Tanaka.

The fat Baron stared down at Barmy. "So you're the boy who destroyed my castle," he said with an unflattering hint of wonder in his voice. "I must say, you don't look as if you have it in you." He shrugged. "Still, I suppose if you're Obedniga's brother. Certain, you will never have that chance again, little man."

"What have you done with the others?" Barmy demanded suddenly. It was not exactly courage, more sudden anger – coupled with the realization he had nothing much to lose, whatever he said now.

"They are perfectly safe, I assure you. Not happy. Not comfortable. Certainly not well fed, but safe and waiting for you to join them."

"And what are you going to do to us?" Barmy demanded.

"Do to you?" asked Tanaka. He smiled without a hint of humour in his eyes. "Do to you, little man? I don't plan to do anything to you." He half turned as if to leave the chamber, then added almost thoughtfully, "I'll leave that to the Ooompatherium."

Behind Barmy, Ben gave a bloodcurdling scream. "Not the Ooompatherium!" he cried. "Anything but the Ooompatherium!"

Chapter Twenty-Seven

They were outside again, in a clearing in a great steaming tangle of jungle swampland. They were tied to individual stakes, great wooden posts that were little more than trimmed tree-trunks, facing the altar but 30 metres or more distant from it. Over to the right, near the edge of the clearing, was a massive wooden framework constructed of notched logs lashed together with leather thongs. Suspended from it was a huge brass bell. And beside the bell, one hand resting loosely on its rope, was a white-robed and hooded figure.

This refugee from the Ku Klux Klan was only one of many hooded figures in the clearing, the outer perimeter of which was ringed by a congregation of ghouls. The figures flitted silent as ghosts, engaged in some complicated ritual observance which involved the burning of the most peculiar incense Barmy had ever smelt.

Barmy looked around him. Ben was tied to a stake. Aspen was tied to a stake. Lancie was tied to a stake. Rowan was tied to a stake. Facecrusher was tied to a stake. Pendragon was tied to a stake. The Amazing Presto was tied to a stake, helpless as a baby, his magic dormant since he could not move his hands. And furtherest from him, his little sister Lauren was tied to a stake, hurling abuse to all and sundry.

Barmy felt a strange surge of affection for Lauren. She had helped him out of a great many difficult situations with her quick wits, her acid tongue and her readiness to savage anything that moved. Earlier, she had even tried to bargain with Tanaka, using the fact that she had once been his war witch. But he was having none of it. Now she was helpless as the others, although considerably louder.

"Keep you spirits up!" called Pendragon bravely. "All is not yet lost."

Barmy ignored him. If he was going to be dead in five minutes, he might as well enjoy being pathetic.

He wondered why everything was so quiet. The last time they had tried to sacrifice him, there had been all sorts of chanting.

One of the robed figures came across and stuffed a gag into Lauren's mouth, so that the scene became even quieter than before. The remainder clumped together and walked through the clearing making curious motions with both hands, as if they were sweeping the ground with invisible brooms. For some reason Barmy felt they might be preparing for a procession.

He was right, as it transpired. The group of sweepers suddenly broke apart and fanned out to take their individual places in a circle round the clearing, just inside the border guard of the ghoul congregation. For a long instant nothing happened, then a flicker of silent movement at the corner of his eye caught his attention.

Barmy twisted his head to discover Tanaka himself had entered the clearing. The Baron was dressed in flowing, sickly-green robes, decorated with rivulets of repulsive pink, a combination which gave him the appearance of a rotting sweet. He wore a tall, winged headdress something similar to a nun's wimple. From a broad belt round his ample waist hung a golden cudgel and an ornamental silver broadsword. He walked with slow dignity, head high, a stupid look of satisfaction pasted on his bloated features.

Grovelling and cringing before Tanaka was a slim priest of the cult with close-set eyes and a shifty expression, who progressed in a series of shuffling steps, some backwards, some sideways like a crab, but all the time watching his master like a beaten dog. This twit was carrying a velvet cushion across which lay the Sceptre of Saul. Barmy noticed at once it was glowing slightly: not just the head, but the entire staff as well. If his theory was correct, the power of the Sceptre was increasing by the day now, perhaps even by the hour. If it could cause a sabre tooth to disappear, and protect Tanaka from Ben's crossbow bolts, heaven alone knew what it might do when it achieved full power. The legends about thunderbolts might even be true.

Tanaka turned to face the captives. "My friends," he said quietly, "I have come to bid you all farewell. You have caused me some small problems in the past, but I forgive you for that now. For you are about to repay me for the trouble a thousandfold." He smiled.

"Why don't you slope off, Tanaka?" Lancie remarked rudely.

"Ah, but that is precisely what I plan to do, Your Holiness," said Tanaka with exaggerated courtesy. "You, however, will not slope off anywhere. You will stay here and await the Ooompatherium."

"Not the Ooompatherium!" Ben cried. "Anything but the Ooompa – " A hooded figure standing near him clapped a hand across his mouth to shut him up.

"Your little friend is right to panic," smiled Tanaka coldly. "When the Ooompatherium arrives, you will surely all be dead within five mintes." He turned to glance fondly at the Sceptre on the altar. "Your life energies will be taken up by this and will then be converted into the most powerful weapon history has ever known."

He turned and swept back the way he had come.

The solitary figure bowed deeply in the direction of the

altar, glanced once at the bound captives, then reached up for the rope.

"The sacrificial hour is here!" he declaimed hollowly. "We call the dreaded Ooompatherium!"

He pulled the rope, then hitched his robes above his knees and ran, his skinny legs pumping like pistons, until he disappeared from view.

The great bell gave out a booming note that reverberated through the jungle like the herald of apocalypse.

Chapter Twenty-Eight

"Ben," asked Barmy rather urgently, "what's an Ooompatherium?"

There was a strangled sob from the next stake. Barmy twisted his head in genuine concern. "It's all right, Ben, there's no nee – " But Ben was not crying: he was laughing. Despite his bonds and their desperate position, he was laughing so much his knees were buckling.

"It's dead!" Ben gasped. "Tanaka thinks the Ooompatherium will eat us, but it's dead! I shot it through the eye and then you frightened it to death by running at it with your axe!"

Barmy's jaw dropped. "The dinosaur? You mean the Ooompatherium is the *dinosaur*?"

"That's right," Ben giggled. "Don't you recognize the swamp, Barmy? This is where it lived. Tanaka feeds people to it when he doesn't like them and it's trained to come when they ring that bell. But we killed it, Barmy! Tanaka doesn't know it yet, but we killed it!" He stamped his little legs up and down in a surfeit of glee.

"You mean we're *safe*?" asked Barmy. He could hardly believe it.

"We're safe!" Ben howled through paroxysms of mirth. "We're safe as houses!"

There was a violent crashing in the undergrowth and a monstrous creature burst into the clearing, great head swinging side to side on the sinuous neck.

Ben stopped laughing. "Unless of course, there's a *second* Ooompatherium," he said.

"Everybody keep perfectly still," ordered Lancelot Bong. "It may not notice us."

"Are you out of your mind?" asked Pendragon. "Of course it will notice us! We're all tied to stakes out in the open!"

"This is obviously a saurian," said the Bong cheerfully. "They're notoriously short-sighted."

"Even if it can't see us, it will scent us," Pendragon insisted.

"Or even hear you talking," Aspen put in quietly.

The Ooompatherium took a couple of steps into the clearing, head swinging pendulously from side to side. The ground shook beneath its tread. It was still more than thirty metres away, but even so, Barmy was forced to look up at it. The monster was the largest living creature he had ever seen, larger than an elephant by far. He found himself comparing it with things like motor coaches, articulated trucks, express trains.

The glittering eyes of the Ooompatherium looked upon them. If it was, as Lancie insisted, short-sighted, it did not seem to know it. The huge jaws opened and it emitted an ear-shattering roar.

"Do your worst!" screamed Pendragon defiantly, ever ready with the useless gesture. "We will die like men!" He glanced across at Aspen and added a little lamely, "And women, of course."

Aspen rolled her eyes to heaven.

The creature was definitely looking straight at Barmy. It began to lumber forward, slavering. Whether he wanted it or not, he was to be eaten first.

Beyond the monster he could see Saul's Sceptre lying on the granite altar.

As he died – assuming Tanaka was correct – his life force would be absorbed to help regenerate the power of the great artifact. And once it was fully active, Tanaka would use it to rule the world.

The brute was half running now, bearing down upon him like an avalanche.

"Grrrr!"

A tan shape hurled itself across the clearing and snapped viciously at the monster's heels. The Ooompatherium stopped its charge at once and swung around, bellowing in surprise. The great head stared down at Eynek who, large though he was, looked like a chihuahua pup beside the monster. Then the Ooompatherium attacked, striking like a snake.

"Eynek – look out!" Rowan screamed in panic.

But as the jaws snapped shut, Eynek was no longer there. Moving with blinding speed, he jumped aside, spun round and –

Hissssss!

"Oh, good grief!" Barmy moaned. Eynek had peed in the dinosaur's eye!

"*Aaaarrrrghhhh!* The monster reared, clawing the air with its shortened forelegs and snapping its head about like a whiplash obviously in considerable pain. Eynek darted in to snap at its back legs once again, then darted away, running like a mad thing towards the clearing's edge. Still pawing at its eye, the Ooompatherium started after him –

And was met with a shower of wooden spears!

"What's going on here?" Barmy asked. Lauren might have worked it out, but she was still gagged and nobody else seemed interested in telling him.

Most of the spears glanced off the armouring that protected the monster's body, although a few shafts insinuated themselves between the scales to penetrate the skin. But they were little more than pinpricks to a brute this size and none was near the vital organs.

147

Eynek changed direction so that the monster was forced to swing round in a circle.

"Run, Eynek!" Rowan roared. "Get out of the clearing, you fool dog!"

But Eynek ignored him. He darted back in, growling, snapped once at the Ooompatherium (and missed) then jumped away again only just in time to avoid the next surge of that massive head. Then they were off again in that ghastly chase, the huge dog racing flat out, the giant saurian lumbering after with earth-shaking strides. It was a mad dog's game, Barmy thought. If Eynek did not get out of the clearing, it was only a matter of time before the dinosaur got him.

And as if to underline the thought, the great head of the Ooompatherium swept across and caught Eynek squarely on the flanks. Eynek yelped and tumbled. Barmy did not think he had been bitten, but when he scrambled to his feet, he was definitely limping. Now it looked as though he would not make it from the clearing even if he tried. In fact it was questionable whether he could still out-distance the brute for long while he remained in the clearing.

The same thought seemed to have occurred to Eynek, for instead of running, he turned at bay, hackles up, teeth bared in hideous challenge. The monster reared above him.

"Noo!" screamed Rowan in an agony of apprehension.

But the dinosaur did not attack. For an eternity it remained poised, then very, very slowly, it began to sink downwards. It was not striking at Eynek, but rather toppling like a tree.

What was happening? Barmy screamed inside his head. *What was happening?* Nothing made much sense any more.

Eynek limped to one side as the Ooompatherium came

crashing down. It was far from dead. The huge head still tried to snap at him, but he remained out of range. Then suddenly the clearing was half-filled with running shapes. Small, lithe figures swarmed on to the dinosaur like ants, hacking and stabbing at the soft parts of its body with a variety of makeshift weapons.

To his astonishment, Barmy recognized the girl-children of the Skangdazzle Tribe.

Chapter Twenty-Nine

"They must have used poison," Aspen murmured. "On their spears. It's the only thing that makes sense."

"Grrr," Eynek confirmed. As the Skangdazzles continued to butcher the paralysed dinosaur, he had limped over to his friends and was trying to untie them with his teeth. Rowan's bonds had proved too much for him and now he was worrying at the knots behind Barmy's back.

"Well," remarked Lancie, "that was a bit of excitement, what?"

"It isn't over yet," Facecrusher said. "I imagine under normal circumstances that thing would have eaten us by now."

"Undoubtedly, dear lady, undoubtedly. However, since this remarkable mutt and those remarkable children – "

"The point," Facecrusher interrupted heavily, "is that my beloved husband may return at any minute. I imagine he would allow a few minutes for us to be eaten, a few more for the monster to get clear, then he would be back to finish the ceremony."

"How right you are, my dear!" said a soft, familiar voice.

Armed ghouls and robed figures were pouring into the clearing. Tanaka stepped into Barmy's field of vision, still dressed in his repulsive ritual robes. His face was white, his neck muscles knotted, like one determined to control a raging fury. Which he probably was, considering the mess the Skangdazzles had made of his pet dinosaur.

"I must confess," Tanaka continued, "I did not anticipate this development. But perhaps it is all to the good.

The Sceptre has absorbed more life force from the Ooom-patherium than it would from all of you put together – "

Barmy's eyes flickered towards the altar. Tanaka was right: the Sceptre was now glowing with a halo of bright blue light, almost dazzling in its intensity.

" – but, of course, it will be absorbing your life force as well in a moment, since you are destined to die by my sword where you stand."

"You wouldn't be so brave if our hands were free, Tanaka!" screamed Pendragon who never seemed to learn. "Why not cut me loose and make a fair fight of it?"

"Why not indeed?" asked Tanaka rhetorically.

"Grrr!"

Despite his limp, Eynek was on Tanaka like a tiger. The Baron went down at once, obviously taken completely by surprise since Eynek had been half hidden behind Barmy before he made his move. As he fell, Tanaka rolled and, moving with surprising agility for a man his bulk, regained his feet with a drawn sword in his hand. "Come on, you brute!" he hissed at Eynek. "Let's see how well you stand up to cold steel!"

"Grrr" said Eynek savagely. But his initial effort seemed to have exaggerated the injury he had already received from the dinosaur, so that he was now moving far more slowly than usual.

The Skangdazzles had abandoned the massive corpse of the Ooompatherium (which actually looked pretty dead by now) and were falling back under a savage onslaught by a huge contingent of ghouls. The little girls were incredible fighters, extrememly fast and utterly ruthless, but sheer weight of numbers was pressing them back.

Tanaka lunged forward. Eynek jumped to one side, but not quite fast enough. He yelped and Barmy saw blood well from a massive slash wound along his side.

151

"Not so snappy now, are you, Ratbag?" Tanaka taunted.

"Grrr!" Eynek attacked again. He was still a fearsome opponent, large and powerful, but he had definitely been slowed. The Baron had little difficulty in avoiding his charge and counterattacked at once, again drawing blood.

Furiously Barmy worked to free the ropes around his wrists.

"Grrr . . ." challenged Eynek, but it was obvious his heart was not entirely in it. He tried to push towards Tanaka, but his legs crumbled beneath him and he lay panting on the ground, eyes rolling in his great head.

The bonds on Barmy's wrists fell away!

For an instant he could hardly believe it had happened, then he hurled himself forward in a fury born of desperation.

"That's your lot, Ratbag!" scowled Tanaka, stepping forward to drive his sword deep into the defenceless body of the prostrate Eynek.

They were too far away! Barmy knew beyond doubt he was not going to make it in time. Nothing, absolutely nothing, could possibly save Eynek now.

The sword plunged, but the exhausted Eynek was no longer panting on the ground helplessly waiting to receive it. He was on his feet again, transformed into a snapping, growling whirlwind that bowled Tanaka over and sent the sword flying from his hand.

"That's it, Eynek!" Rowan yelled from his stake. "The old possum trick fools them every time!"

The Skangdazzles broke before the ghoul onslaught, but instead of fighting a formal retreat, they simply melted into the undergrowth outside the clearing. The ghouls blundered after them, hacking and howling, but finding nothing of any interest underneath their swords.

Out of the corner of his eye, Barmy could see a group

of hooded figures moving towards his bound companions, long, curved sacrificial knives glinting in their hands. He needed no one to tell him what that meant.

Eynek had Tanaka on the ground, robes firmly gripped, and was shaking him savagely. Barmy changed direction slightly and ran right past them. Even if Eynek had the upper hand – paw – on Tanaka, nothing else was going right. Unless he could manage something spectacular within the next few seconds, his friends would be dead, the Skangdazzles routed and Eynek dragged off the Baron by the small army of ghouls even now bearing down on them.

A ghoul appeared in his path, waving a sword, Barmy ducked beneath the weapon and stiff-fingered the creature in the throat without even pausing in his stride. He shouldered between two more ghouls before they realized what was happening, then vaulted up on to the granite altar.

For an instant he hesitated, then reached down and took up the glowing Sceptre. At once the power flooded through him like a swollen river. The glow of the Sceptre transferred itself to his body and electrical torrents began to flicker like extended fingers from his hands and arms. He felt as if he was growing, but so quickly that his skin must burst. The full energy of the Ooompatherium erupted suddenly within his body and he felt as if he could leap high buildings in a single stride or smash through walls with his bare hands.

"Stop!" he roared in a voice that seemed to reverberate throughout the universe. "Stop! Stop! STOP!" He raised the Sceptre aloft.

From high above a massive thunderbolt smashed down into the centre of the clearing, gouging out a crater deep enough to swallow up another Ooompatherium and scattering debris in all directions.

"Stop!" Barmy called again; and suddenly the ghouls and hooded figures vanished.

Slowly he lowered the Sceptre. Not a ghoul remained. Not a hooded human was in sight. Eynek was still shaking his head, but there was no longer a Tanaka in his mouth. He stopped and looked around him in bewilderment.

Barmy climbed down from the altar. One by one the Skangdazzles emerged into the clearing, glancing around suspiciously. Barmy dropped the glowing Sceptre. It was over. The Baron was defeated. It had all happened so quickly, his companions had not yet taken it in, but it had happened. Tanaka was gone, blasted into oblivion or transported heaven only knew where by the power of the Sceptre. They were safe.

He walked across to Lauren and removed the gag from her mouth. "You took your time," she said. But for the first time he could remember, there was admiration in her eyes.

Chapter Thirty

They had decorated the Keep with flags and bunting. Two brass bands and the marching pipes were out, each playing different tunes. A hefty crowd had emerged on to the green, sufficiently large to encourage several merchants to set up stalls and some jugglers to try to make money from impromptu entertainment. Barmy found it all very embarrassing, although Lauren seemed to enjoy it, bowing and smiling as they strolled together towards the Möbius strip.

The Bong was heading up the dignitaries, flanked by the Vampire Mayor, now no longer vampire since the thing that bit him had been staked. He looked none the worse for his experience, except that he was considerably thinner. Nobody had remembered to release him from the wicker cage for a long time after he had recovered.

Besides the dignitaries, in a tight little group, stood Aspen, Ben, Pendragon, Facecrusher, the Amazing Presto and the entire Skangdazzle Tribe, scrubbed for the occasion and now dressed in neat, matching linen tunics.

A little way from the group sat Eynek, ears erect, tail twitching. His ribs and one of his back legs were bandaged and he had several bits of sticking plaster on his head, but otherwise he looked none the worse for wear. Rowan was leaning nonchalantly against him.

The Bong strode forward. "I told them not to worry about speeches," he said to Barmy's relief. "Goodbyes are difficult enough without them, what?"

Barmy nodded, suddenly aware of a lump in his throat.

"Goodbye, Barmy," Aspen called from the group. "Goodbye Lauren." She grinned and waved.

"Goodbye," Barmy called. "Goodbye everybody." He knew he would have to get through the warp and back home quickly before he broke down altogether. "Come on, Lauren," he whispered.

But as they reached the warp, Eynek suddenly bounded towards them, leaping up so quickly that Rowan actually fell over.

"Grrr," Eynek said, nuzzling Barmy with his nose. Lauren put an arm around his neck and kissed his ear. "We'll miss you too," she said.

Barmy frowned, wondering how it was everybody could understand exactly what Eynek was saying except him. Although maybe she just guessed.

Rowan materialized beside them. "You're going to have to come back, you know," he grinned.

"Are we?" Barmy asked, feeling a sudden lift in his spirits.

"No doubt about it," Rowan said. He winked and placed a finger along one side of his nose. "Unfinished business."

"What's that?" Barmy asked. Out of the corner of his eye he saw that Ben had broken away from the group and was approaching stolidly.

Rowan dropped his voice. "The Tomb of Tarantulus," he whispered. "We know where it is now; and we're the only ones in the world who do . . ."

"Yes, we are, aren't we?" Barmy grinned suddenly.

"There's enough treasure in that place to make us all rich," Rowan said.

"Rich beyond the dreams of avarice," said Ben, having arrived. He paused, then added thoughtfully, "I'd like to be rich beyond dreams of avarice, Barmy. Wouldn't you?"

"I don't know, Ben," Barmy said truthfully. But he did know one thing: he wanted to come back – and badly. "Goodbye Rowan," he said softly. "Goodbye Eynek. Goodbye Ben. We'll see you soon." He took Lauren's hand and they both fell at once into the weird contortions of the Quasimodo Walk.

Together they walked into the Möbius Warp and disappeared.

GRAIL QUEST

Solo Fantasy Gamebooks

J. H. Brennan

King Arthur's magic realm of Avalon is besieged on every side by evil powers and foul monsters. You alone can free the kingdom from its terror, venturing forth on Quests too deadly for even the bold Knights of the Round Table. Quests that will lead you to glory — or death.

So sharpen your wits and your trusty sword Excalibur Junior, and use the intricate combat system to scheme and fight your way through the adventures in this thrilling gamebook series. A special score card and detachable easy-reference rules bookmark are included with each book.

The Castle of Darkness	**The Den of Dragons**
The Gateway of Doom	**Voyage of Terror**
Kingdom of Horror	**Realm of Chaos**
Tomb of Nightmares	**Legion of the Dead**

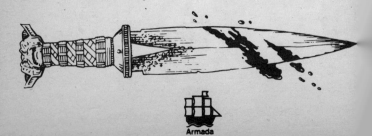

Armada

Horror Classic Gamebooks
by J. H. Brennan

Now you can bring your favourite horror characters
to life in these spinechilling gamebooks.

Dracula's Castle

Deadly traps and evil cunning await Jonathan Harker on
his arrival at the forbidding Castle Dracula. The choice
is yours whether to play the fearless vampire-hunter or
his arch-enemy, the vampire count himself. Will you
have the stamina to survive?

The Curse of Frankenstein

Enter the ghoulish world of Frankenstein and his
monstrous creation. But be warned, you will need skill,
luck and nerves of steel to endure this bloodcurdling
adventure.

Armada

Armadas

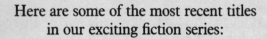

Here are some of the most recent titles
in our exciting fiction series:

The Chalet School and Rosalie *Elinor M. Brent-Dyer* £1.75
The Secret of the Forgotten City *Carolyn Keene* £1.95
The Masked Monkey *Franklin W. Dixon* £1.95
The Mystery of the Creep-Show Crooks *M. V. Carey* £1.95
Horse of Fire *Patricia Leitch* £1.75
Cry of a Seagull *Monica Dickens* £1.75
The Secret of Moon Castle *Enid Blyton* £1.95
Legion of the Dead *J. H. Brennan* £1.95

Armada paperbacks are available in
bookshops and newsagents, but can
also be ordered by post.

How to Order

Please send the purchase price plus 22p per book (maximum postal charge £3.00) to Armada Paperbacks, Cash Sales Dept., GPO Box 29, Douglas, Isle of Man. Please use cheque, postal or money order – do not send currency.

NAME (Block letters) ....

ADDRESS ....

....

....